CONTENTS

INTRODUCTION

The Vietnam War, as it is known in America, or the American War, as it is known in Vietnam, lasted nearly twenty years and claimed more than two million lives. It began quietly, when President Dwight D. Eisenhower sent supplies and American advisers to assist the government of South Vietnam in their struggle against the **Communist** North Vietnamese. It would end tragically, with a nation destroyed by war, with tens of thousands of Americans killed and billions of U.S. dollars spent.

And yet, had you predicted in 1955 that a small country on the other end of the world would be the battleground for one of the ugliest conflicts in American history, no one would have believed you. Most Americans would have been unlikely to find the country on a map. It had almost no historic or political ties to the United States. What possible reason did the U.S. have to go to war there?

The story of how Vietnam went from being a country Americans were unaware of to a graveyard for many tens of thousands of them is part of the story of this book. But it isn't the whole story. The Vietnam conflict was fought by millions of people. Its beginnings can be traced back decades before the U.S. arrived, and its aftereffects are still being felt today.

Each of the six men featured in this book saw the Vietnam

THE VIETNAM WAR

By Daniel Polansky

Ngo Dinh Diem

John F. Kennedy

Ho Chi Minh

Lyndon B. Johnson

William Westmoreland

Henry Kissinger

SCHOLASTIC INC.

....

conflict in different terms. Some saw it as a struggle for national independence, others as part of a political chess game being played between the United States and the Soviet Union. By learning about each of them in turn, we begin to gain a broader picture of the conflict.

For Ngo Dinh Diem, the first president of Vietnam after it gained independence from France, American intervention in Vietnam was an opportunity to ensure that Vietnam developed into the country that he wished it to be. One that was noncommunist, dominated by a **Catholic** minority, and ruled carefully by himself and his immediate family. His inability to think of South Vietnam in larger terms, as a country that served the needs of its entire people, was the reason for his demise. Indeed, it would prove to be one of the fundamental problems facing South Vietnam during the conflict.

For President John F. Kennedy, Vietnam was one relatively small part of the greater issue of his time: the ongoing struggle against the Soviet Union. Vietnam itself only mattered as part of this conflict between the free world, led by the United States, and the Communist world, led by the Soviet Union. Kennedy believed that if Communism was not stopped in Vietnam, it would spread throughout East Asia, to Cambodia, Vietnam, Japan, and India. To prevent this, he was willing to introduce American troops

into the civil war that raged between North and South
Vietnamese.

For Ho Chi Minh, the leader of North Vietnam, the
conflict with the U.S. was one stage in a lifelong struggle
to gain independence for his country. He fought the French,
the Japanese, and the Chinese to make Vietnam an
independent nation, playing each against the other in turn.
The U.S. was simply the next in line, one more enemy to be
defeated by the patient, gradual, and effective means that
his forces had perfected.

For President Lyndon B. Johnson, Vietnam was a
distraction that became a catastrophe. He came into office
hoping to advance the social programs that were dear to
his heart. To help bring the poor out of poverty, provide
comfort to the weak, and make the United States a more
just and decent nation were his ambitions. But Vietnam
would become the issue that defined his presidency.
Unable to win the war and unwilling to give up, Vietnam
was his downfall. Ultimately, Johnson was so sickened
and disheartened by the conflict that he ended a lifelong
political career rather than continue to help the fight.

For U.S. General William Westmoreland, Vietnam was
a war like any other, no different from the conflicts he
had fought during World War II and the Korean War.
There was an enemy to be defeated, and it was his job

to find a method to beat them. So long as the American public remained committed to the war, he believed that American superiority in training and equipment would inevitably result in victory. But he failed to appreciate the greater political aspects of war. The sacrifices the North Vietnamese were willing to make to free their country of foreign rule were far greater than the ones the American public was willing to make to continue to support the South Vietnamese government.

For U.S. Secretary of State Henry Kissinger, Vietnam was a problem to be solved. It was an obstacle to the new world he wanted to exist: a world in which the Soviet Union and the United States each accepted the other and worked to find areas of cooperation rather than conflict. To advance his goals, he was willing to take enormous political risks, and to unleash upon Vietnam and its neighbors even more terrible levels of violence than they had ever seen.

For the more than two million men and women who died during the conflict, and for their families and loved ones, the war was a tragedy, plain and simple. By learning the history of the war, we do honor to their memories. By understanding the causes of the war, we gain an appreciation for the ways in which small conflicts can escalate into complicated and unexpected catastrophes.

NGO DINH DIEM

NGO DINH DIEM was the first president of South Vietnam. An anticommunist, the U.S. supported his government in the fight against North Vietnam. He implemented biased and oppressive policies against his people. He was eventually assassinated and his government was overthrown.

EARLY LIFE

Vietnam is an ancient country with a turbulent history. At the southern tip of mainland Asia, it has spent thousands of years fighting to avoid becoming a part of the Chinese Empire. But after a series of wars in the mid-1800s, Vietnam had become a territory of the French Empire. Although technically the country was still ruled by a Vietnamese emperor, he had very little actual power, and was not able to make any important decisions. The French controlled the country's military, ran the government, and took most of the wealth. The Vietnamese people were largely rice farmers, following ancient agricultural practices with the changing of the seasons. The vast majority were **Buddhist** and their culture emphasized the importance of family, duty, and loyalty to one's village.

In many ways, Ngo Dinh Diem was not your typical Vietnamese person. He was born in 1901, in the city of Hue; he was the third of six

Map of Vietnam

sons. His family had converted to Catholicism several generations earlier, and Diem was a devoted follower of that religion. His father, Ngo Dinh Kha, was a close adviser of the Vietnamese emperor, called a Mandarin. In 1907, the French decided to overthrow the Vietnamese emperor, who was showing signs that he wanted to take more control over his country. Diem's father resigned in protest, leaving the city to become a rice farmer.

Life became much harder for Diem after that, and Diem had to split his time between working in the rice fields and attending school. He was a talented student—hard working and intelligent. At one point he briefly considered becoming a priest, like his elder brother, but ultimately decided against it. Instead, he moved to Hanoi, a major city in the north of Vietnam. There he enrolled in the School of Law and Administration, a French-run academy that prepared students to work in the government. After graduating he entered the **civil service**.

Diem showed great talent as an administrator, quickly rising through the ranks. He worked as a **rural** governor, making sure that the small villages in the countryside he controlled were well run, and the peasants were properly taken care of. It was as a governor that Diem first came in contact with Communism. Communism is a political philosophy created by Karl Marx, a German philosopher.

It argues that a **capitalist** society is unjust, and that the future of human civilization is one in which factory workers and farmers make political decisions.

Communism became a powerful idea, one that inspired revolutionary activities throughout the world. Rural Vietnam had a strong Communist presence, especially in the North. Many thousands of Communist supporters worked to convert the peasants to Communism. They distributed pro-Communist pamphlets and criticized the ruling French government. Diem quickly became a vocal anticommunist. He wrote and distributed his own pamphlets against Communism. He also worked to find and arrest the Communist supporters within his area.

Despite his success, Diem's political career was hurt because he was an outspoken Vietnamese **Nationalist**, meaning that he believed Vietnam should be run by the Vietnamese, not the French. In 1933, the young French emperor, Bao Dai, officially took the throne, but it was still the French government making all of the important decisions. The French

Karl
Marx

offered Diem the position of minister of the interior under the new emperor. Diem asked if Bao Dai would have real power, or if he would be controlled by the French. He was told to "take the job, and don't complain."

Diem took the job, but he left after only three months, angry at the French refusal to allow the Vietnamese political freedom. As punishment, Diem was stripped of his medals and threatened with arrest.

Diem spent the next ten years outside of politics, living quietly with his family. In 1940, as part of their expansion

Emperor Bao Dai

during World War II, the Japanese invaded Vietnam, easily
defeating the small French army. At first, Diem, along with
many of his countrymen, was hopeful that the Japanese
would help the Vietnamese set up a free government. But
the Japanese were no more interested in allowing the
Vietnamese to control their country than were the French.
They set up a puppet government, like the French had, and
stripped Vietnam of its wealth.

At the end of World War II, the Japanese were defeated
by U.S. and their allies, and left Vietnam in 1945. The
French quickly returned, hoping to regain the power
they had lost. But having been so easily beaten by the
Japanese, the French no longer seemed so impressive.
Many Vietnamese became convinced that the time was
right for a revolution that would allow them to regain
control of their country. In North Vietnam, where French
power was weakest, Communist Vietnamese forces led by
Ho Chi Minh announced the creation of the Democratic
Republic of Vietnam. His forces were commonly known as
the Vietminh. They swore to fight until the French were
forced out. It was the beginning of what is now called the
First Indochina War, and it lasted nine long years.

Diem was torn. He was a passionate Nationalist, and
wanted the French out of Vietnam as much as anyone. But
he was also very strongly anticommunist. Not only was he

against the idea of Communism, but two of Diem's brothers
had already been killed by the Vietminh, which made the
issue very personal. Diem started a political organization
that was against both the Vietminh and the French. It
was ineffective, but his anticommunist stance angered the
Vietminh. Late in 1945, Diem was captured while traveling
in the north of Vietnam and imprisoned for six months.
Eventually, he was taken to meet Ho Chi Minh, who tried
to convince him to join the Communists. Diem refused, and
out of respect for Diem's courage, Ho Chi Minh ordered his
release.

EXILE AND RISE TO POWER

Diem moved south, to Saigon, later the capital of South
Vietnam. He continued his political activities, but he had
little success. Frustrated by his lack of progress, and
fearful that the Vietminh might assassinate him, Diem
left Vietnam. He traveled to Japan, then to Italy, and
then to the United States. He spent years working in a
Catholic seminary in New Jersey. While in the U.S., he
made friends with many influential American political and
religious leaders. Still, it seemed that despite all of his hard
work, Diem would never again hold an important political
position.

But a strange turn of events thrust Diem back into

the spotlight. For nine years, between 1945 and 1954, the French and the Vietminh fought a bitter war for control of Vietnam. It was a conflict that would later have unfortunate similarities with America's own struggle in Vietnam. The French had equipment that the Vietminh lacked, like tanks, airplanes, and heavy artillery. But they had no political support amongst the Vietnamese peasants, and they were unable to hold on to a territory after conquering it. The French people also began to tire of the war, seeing it as a pointless waste of lives and money.

Ngo Dinh Diem, 1955

In short, the French wanted out of Vietnam.

Although the United States did not have any troops fighting in the First Indochina War, they gave the French army many billions of dollars in supplies and equipment. They were afraid that if Vietnam became a Communist country, a wave of similar revolutions would take place throughout the region. Without really meaning to, the U.S. had taken over as being the primary backer of anticommunist South Vietnam.

In 1954, a conference was called in Geneva, Switzerland. There the French, American, Chinese, Soviet, British, Cambodian, Laotian, and Vietnamese governments would try to come up with a way to end the fighting in Vietnam. It was very difficult, as all of the different countries involved wanted different things, and in many ways, the Vietnamese diplomats were the least powerful. The Geneva Accords officially split Vietnam into two different countries. The Communists controlled the North, while the South would be run by the Emperor Bao Dai and backed by French and U.S. power. Diem was to be Bao Dai's chief adviser. It seemed that the terrible violence that plagued Vietnam had finally come to an end. In fact, it was just beginning.

HEAD OF SOUTH VIETNAM

Although Diem was now prime minister, his position was

very weak. Vietnam was split into two halves. In the North, the Vietminh were furious at the results of the Geneva Accords. They felt that they had defeated the French on the battlefield but lost at the negotiating table. They also saw the new country of South Vietnam as being America's "puppet state," meaning a state governed by an outside authority. They saw this as no different from when it had been occupied by the French.

Many of those living in what was now North Vietnam were frightened of being part of a Communist country. After the signing of the Geneva Accords, a million North Vietnamese people, mainly Catholics, fled to South Vietnam. Having to feed and care for this huge group put tremendous pressure on the South Vietnamese government.

Prime Minister Diem

Diem's political position was also very weak. Although Emperor Bao Dai had made Diem his prime minister, he didn't trust Diem. They frequently argued about who would ultimately decide questions of government policy. The Emperor was also very corrupt. He had

Diem at his presidential inauguration

close ties to Vietnamese criminal groups. The emperor allowed them to operate freely in Saigon, the capital city of South Vietnam. In return, they paid the Emperor and promised to use their army of fighters to support him.

But Diem was an excellent schemer, and proved to be smarter and more skilled than the Emperor. First, he gradually put his own people into positions of power throughout the military and the government. Then he arranged a confrontation between his loyal army supporters and the criminal organizations that backed the emperor. A battle raged throughout Saigon, but at the end of it, Diem's forces were victorious.

Diem's next step was to hold an election in South Vietnam to determine whether he or Bao Dai would be the country's supreme ruler. The elections were extremely unfair. His supporters threatened voters, and in some cases actually stuffed ballot boxes. Diem claimed to have won 98.2 percent of the vote, an unbelievable number that only emphasized the dishonest nature of the elections. But there was nothing that Bao Dai could do. Diem's clever maneuvering had made him the head of the government of South Vietnam.

But Diem's troubles were far from over. Much of the country considered him an undeserving ruler. His own generals were constantly scheming to overthrow him and adopt power. Beyond all that, the North Vietnamese continued to be the biggest problem facing Diem. One part of the Geneva Accords called for free elections in North and South Vietnam, with the results determining which government would take over and reunite the countries. But Diem delayed, and then canceled the vote, fearing that free elections would allow the Communists to come to power. The North Vietnamese were, of course, furious. They began to give military assistance to Communist soldiers from South Vietnam, who were nicknamed the Vietcong. The Vietcong raided villages and tried to push out the South Vietnamese army.

Diem's **regime** relied on the financial and political support of the U.S., who provided him with money and military advisers. In return, they expected that Diem would follow U.S. advice in deciding how to govern, and

The South Vietnamese president and his family

particularly in making decisions regarding the Vietcong. But Diem was resistant to U.S. suggestions. He did not want to be seen as just another puppet of a foreign power. He was also fearful for his own security, and did not want to give power to people he didn't trust. He had good reason to be afraid, as several attempts were made to assassinate him. Increasingly, Diem grew to rely entirely on his immediate family, giving them important positions within the government.

By 1961, the Vietcong had become a powerful military presence in the rural portions of South Vietnam. They attacked small military positions, and they had a major presence in the villages, where they intimidated anticommunist peasants. To guard against this, Diem began what was called the Strategic Hamlet Program. In it, Vietnamese peasants were removed from their villages and sent to hamlets. The hamlets were basically small towns with walls and other defensive structures. The idea was that with the peasants living within these hamlets, the army could better protect them from raids by the North Vietnamese than if they were spread all throughout the countryside.

The program proved to be incredibly unpopular. The peasants hated being forced to leave their homes and the graves of their ancestors. The Strategic Hamlets were often not built correctly, or lacked the supplies they were supposed to have, a result of the corruption that was everywhere in the South

Diem, 1962

John F. Kennedy

Vietnamese government. In short, the Strategic Hamlet Program was a disaster, pushing many Vietnamese peasants into the hands of the Communists. It was also a tremendous waste of money. By 1963, it had been all but abandoned.

The Strategic Hamlet Program, like most of the rest of the South Vietnamese government's activities, was paid for with American money, on the orders of President Kennedy. Kennedy found himself in a very difficult position, one that would repeat itself throughout the coming conflict in Vietnam. Kennedy disliked and distrusted Diem. He recognized that Diem was more interested in gaining personal power than in fighting the Communists in the North, and he was angered by Diem's refusal to listen to the recommendations made to him by his American advisers. But Kennedy also did not see any alternative to continuing to support him. He feared the spread of Communism, and was worried that

Diem's replacement would be an even worse leader. Also, he did not really understand the complex and secretive style of Vietnamese politics, another problem that would affect America's activities in the years to come.

OVERTHROW AND DEATH

Despite working his whole life to gain power, Diem ended up being a very bad leader. He was corrupt and incompetent, giving authority to his family and ignoring the well-being of the country. He angered the Vietnamese people by passing laws that they did not agree with and by using his political power to make himself and his relatives rich. In particular, Diem gave unfair advantages to the country's minority Catholic population, of which Diem was a part. Catholics were put into positions of power in the government and military. Diem also refused to allow Buddhists to take part in their traditional religious holidays.

Although many people were unhappy with Diem's rule, it would be the backlash against his anti-Buddhist policies that would ultimately lead to his downfall. In May 1963, in the city of Hue, a celebration marking the 2527th birthday of the Buddha was to take place. The governor of the city, following Diem's anti-Buddhist policies, refused to allow the celebration. When the Buddhists went forward with their parades anyway, the governor had his troops shoot into the

President Diem at an interview during Buddhist uprisings

crowd, killing nine people. The shooting sparked protests by Buddhist monks and supporters throughout Vietnam.

The U.S. was appalled. President Kennedy told his ambassadors to make it clear that they would not continue to support Diem if he continued his anti-Buddhist policies. But Diem refused to listen, falsely insisting that the Buddhist protesters were part of a Communist conspiracy. Diem was growing increasingly delusional, seeing conspiracies everywhere, and unable to trust anyone outside his family.

In fact, there were many people plotting and scheming to take over the government from Diem, and they recognized that it was the time to strike. The nation was furious at his anti-Buddhist policies, as well as his personal corruption. The U.S. was also angered by Diem's inability to successfully fight the Vietcong rebels. A group of Vietnamese generals, led by Duong Van Minh, began to lay the plans that would lead to the downfall of Ngo Dinh Diem.

For the conspiracy to succeed, the generals knew that they would need the support of the U.S. But this was not so easy to get. There was great disagreement among President Kennedy's advisers as to what should be done. Diem turned out to be corrupt, incompetent, and immoral. But there was no reason to think whoever took over for him would be any better. At the same time, the U.S. did not want to support a leader whom the country hated. Ultimately, the U.S. decided that they would not do anything to actively stop Duong Van Minh and the other conspirators from overthrowing Diem.

On November 1, 1963, Minh and the other generals surrounded the palace and demanded that Diem resign. At first, Diem tried to escape, but ultimately he agreed to give himself up on the condition that he would not be hurt. This condition would not be kept   though it is unclear who exactly was responsible for the order, Diem was murdered shortly after surrendering to the generals.

Kennedy and his American advisers were horrified. They

Ngo Dinh Diem's
unmarked grave

had not anticipated that Diem would be murdered when they agreed to allow the mission to take place. In a tragic twist of fate, Kennedy himself would be assassinated only a short time later.

Ultimately, like many men throughout history, Diem had discovered that gaining power is far easier than using it well. His own tremendous ambitions, which had driven him to fight for power throughout his life, were what led to his downfall.

But Diem's death would be just the first of many changes in the leadership of South Vietnam. The generals responsible for murdering him and taking power were soon overthrown as well: a cycle that would continue throughout the remainder of America's military involvement in Vietnam. Eventually, the U.S. would be forced to nearly run the country itself. This was one of the great difficulties the U.S. faced in Vietnam. The Communist forces were united. They did not argue or lose sight of their overriding mission. The rulers of South Vietnam were more interested in their own power than they were in the future of their country. Their refusal, or inability, to lead proved to be perhaps the biggest obstacle in America's war in Vietnam.

JOHN F. KENNEDY

JOHN FITZGERALD KENNEDY was the thirty-fifth president of the United States. Fearful of the spread of Communism, he sent U.S. funds and military troops to support the South Vietnamese government during the Vietnam War. He would not live to the see the war's conclusion, however, as he was assassinated in 1963 in Dallas, Texas.

EARLY LIFE

John Fitzgerald Kennedy was born in Brookline, Massachusetts, on May 29, 1917. He was the second son of Joseph P. Kennedy, Sr., and Rose Fitzgerald, born two years after Joe, the eldest. In time, six more children would become part of the Kennedy family, five sisters and two brothers: Rosemary, Kathleen, Eunice, Patricia, Robert, Jean Ann, and Edward.

Jack, as he was called by his friends and family, was born into one of the most powerful political families in Massachusetts. His mother's father was a three-term mayor of Boston, and later a congressman. His father was an extremely successful businessman with close ties to the **Democratic** Party. At one point he was even made the U.S. ambassador to England.

John F. Kennedy as a baby

Kennedy's early life was happy. His family was close and wealthy. They spent summers in his family's mansion in Hyannis Port, Massachusetts, and Christmas at their winter home in Palm Beach, Florida. In school, Kennedy was an energetic and sometimes even mischievous child.

He often felt like he was in the shadow of his older brother, Joe, who was an excellent athlete and student. His behavior probably stemmed from a desire to distinguish himself. Despite his youthful rebelliousness, Kennedy was still very active, being treasurer of the school yearbook, and playing football and other sports. In fact, it was while playing football that Kennedy ruptured a disc in his back. It was a serious injury that never healed correctly, and caused him great pain throughout the rest of his life.

Kennedy at ten years old

After graduating from high school in 1935, Kennedy entered Harvard University. Once there he began to take his studies more seriously, majoring in science and developing an interest in political philosophy. In part because of his father's position as ambassador, Kennedy closely followed the buildup to what would become World War II. He strongly believed that England should have done more to stop the rise of Nazi Germany before it became too powerful. He even wrote his college thesis on it, which would later be published as a book called *Why England Slept*. He believed that backing down during an international conflict would only lead to trouble. It was a belief he carried with him into his future political career and one that would affect his decisions during Vietnam.

Shortly after graduating from college, Kennedy decided to enter the military. His injured back made him ineligible for service in the U.S. Army, so he joined the U.S. Navy instead. After the Japanese Empire bombed Pearl Harbor on December 7, 1941, Kennedy was made a lieutenant and was assigned to command a patrol torpedo boat in the South Pacific.

During the night of August 2, 1943, while patrolling for enemy craft, Kennedy's boat was unexpectedly rammed by a Japanese destroyer, a type of ship much larger than the small patrol boat Kennedy commanded. Kennedy's boat was broken in two, and several of his men were killed. The rest of Kennedy's crew were floating on the other half of the patrol boat. Kennedy was an excellent swimmer, having spent many hours in the pool, in part as therapy for his bad back. He led his men to a nearby island. At one point he even towed an injured sailor by biting down onto the man's life jacket strap while swimming. Kennedy and his

U.S. naval officer
John F. Kennedy in
South Pacific, 1943

men were rescued after spending six days on the island. As a result of that ordeal, Kennedy's back injury worsened. In later years he would undergo many operations in hopes of easing his pain, all without much success.

For his conduct in saving the lives of his men, Kennedy was awarded the U.S. Navy and Marine Corps Medal. Kennedy always kept a sense of humor about his actions during the war. When asked how he became a war hero, he later joked, "It was easy. They cut my PT boat in half."

ENTERING POLITICS

Kennedy's older brother, Joe, had always been the one his family expected to enter politics. When he was killed in action in Europe during World War II, Kennedy decided he needed to carry on his family's legacy. In 1946 he ran for

Congress in Massachusetts as a Democrat. He won easily. He spent three terms as a congressman, serving for a total of six years. In 1952 he ran for the Senate and won.

Despite his political success, Kennedy's life was far from easy during this period. He had to undergo several major surgeries to his spinal cord and was frequently sick, at one point even near death. It was while recovering from back surgery that Kennedy wrote *Profiles in Courage*, a book praising the courage and nobility of eight prominent U.S. senators. It won him the Pulitzer Prize for a biography, became a worldwide bestseller, and made the general U.S. public aware of him.

During his time in congress, Kennedy met Jacqueline Bouvier, a young socialite. They were married in Newport, Rhode Island, in 1953. "Jackie," as she was more commonly known, was a stylish and beautiful woman. She would become immensely popular as a First Lady and later on as a celebrity and philanthropist in her

Kennedy and Bouvier cutting the cake at their wedding, 1953

own right. The couple had two children, Caroline and John Fitzgerald, Jr.

In 1960, Kennedy began his campaign for president. After overcoming opposition in the primaries, Kennedy chose Lyndon Baines Johnson of Texas, the senate majority leader and a veteran southern Democrat, as his vice presidential nominee.

One of the difficulties Kennedy faced during his election campaign was his religion. Kennedy was a practicing

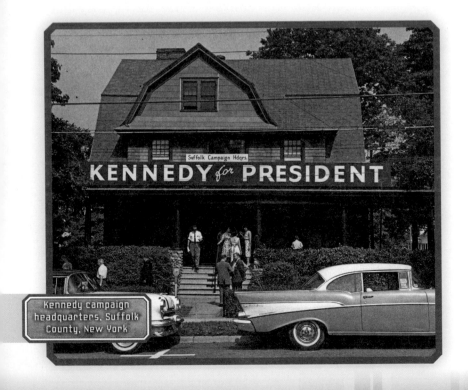

Kennedy campaign headquarters, Suffolk County, New York

Roman Catholic. At that time in America there was a great deal of anti-Catholic bias. Some peopled believed that Catholics could not be trusted in political office because their religion required obedience to the **Pope**. At a meeting of the Greater Houston Ministerial Association, Kennedy gave a now famous speech in which he defended religious freedom. In it, Kennedy promised that he would put the needs of the nation ahead of his religious beliefs. He also criticized his opponents for questioning his patriotism and the patriotism of his fellow Catholics despite all they had done for the country. The speech is now seen as a critical moment in American history. It helped convince the public that a presidential candidate can be of any religion.

Another noteworthy event during Kennedy's campaign was the first televised presidential debate, held between

Vice President Richard Nixon and Senator John F. Kennedy during a televised presidential debate

him and his **Republican** opponent, Vice President Richard Milhous Nixon. Nixon was an experienced politician and a skilled debater. However, he did not fully appreciate the ways in which a televised debate was different from other debate forums. During the debates, Kennedy looked cool and calm. Nixon seemed tense and uncomfortable. Although people listening on the radio thought the debate was a draw, the television audience saw Kennedy as the clear victor. These debates were of great historical importance, marking the period when television began to become a dominant factor in American politics.

Despite his successful debate performance, the election was extremely close. Kennedy won 49.7 percent of the popular vote, with Nixon taking 49.5 percent. It was the closest election of the twentieth century.

PRESIDENCY

Kennedy took the inaugural oath on January 20, 1961, becoming our nation's thirty-fifth president. At the age of forty-three, he became the youngest person to ever hold the office. His inaugural address spoke of the need for all Americans to sacrifice for the betterment of the country. It included his now famous appeal to "ask not what your country can do for you, but what you can do for your country."

President Kennedy in the Oval Office

Despite his optimism, America faced many challenges. Domestically, the country was divided to a degree that it had not been since perhaps the Civil War. In particular, this tension centered on the issue of segregation, which was the legal separation of U.S. citizens according to race. Kennedy was sympathetic toward advancing the cause of civil rights. However, he was concerned that large protests would result in a backlash that would make it more difficult to pass civil rights legislation. At that time a good portion of the Democratic Party was made up of pro-segregation southerners. He feared if he pushed too hard on civil rights he would lose their support. In 1963, Kennedy decided that the time had come for action. He proposed the Civil Rights Act, which outlawed segregation in public places.

Kennedy's other major domestic policies included creating the Peace Corps, an organization that sends U.S. volunteers to work in **developing countries**. He was also the first president to call for heavy investment in spaceflight technology, promising to put a man on the moon within ten years. It was a dream he would not live to see fulfilled.

Internationally, Kennedy faced some of the most serious issues to ever confront the country. The main one being how to deal with the rising power of the Soviet Union, which consisted of Communist Russia and many surrounding republics. Although the Soviet Union and the United States had been **allies** during World War II, in the years since, an atmosphere of great fear and tension had developed between the two great superpowers. The Soviet Union had gradually expanded its control over Eastern and Central Europe until it dominated half of the continent. The U.S.

Map of the USSR and surrounding Communist countries

and the Soviets were continually bickering about the fate of Germany, which had been divided into two separate countries, one Democratic and one Communist. Outside of Europe, Communism seemed to be spreading quickly as well, with China becoming a Communist country in 1949.

This period of conflict between the "free" and Communist

powers was called the Cold War. While there would never be any direct fighting, both sides worked to limit and decrease the other's power. Many people in the U.S., and throughout the noncommunist world, feared the continual growth of Communism. What made the Cold War so terrifying for many at the time was that both the U.S. and the Soviet Union had developed a large supply of **nuclear weapons**. It seemed possible that even a minor disagreement could ignite a full-scale nuclear war. The results of such a war would be catastrophic for the entire world.

Perhaps the closest the two countries ever came to a nuclear war occurred shortly after Kennedy took office, during the Cuban Missile Crisis. In 1959 the country of Cuba, an island only ninety miles from Florida, was taken over by Communist forces. Worried about having a Communist country so close to the United States, Kennedy sent a small army of American-trained Cubans to try and overthrow the Communist government. The invasion was a disaster; the troops were captured or killed soon after landing in Cuba.

The Soviet Union was furious at Kennedy's attempt to invade their ally, and responded by planning to put nuclear missiles in Cuba. This was unacceptable to the U.S. Kennedy announced that any attempt by the Soviet Union to send missiles to Cuba would be blocked by the

MEDIUM RANGE BALLISTIC MISSILE BASE IN CUBA
SAN CRISTOBAL

LAUNCH POSITION

MISSILE-READY TENTS

MISSILE ERECTORS

Aerial view of San Cristóbal, Cuba, 1962

U.S. Navy. It seemed the unthinkable might happen, and the two superpowers would go to war. But Kennedy and the Soviet leader, Nikita Khrushchev, negotiated a compromise by which the U.S. would promise never to again attempt to invade Cuba, and the Soviets would agree not to put missiles in Cuba. Nuclear war was narrowly avoided, but the crisis showed just how tense the Cold War had become.

VIETNAM

For Kennedy, the spread of Communism in Vietnam was one "battle" in the ongoing Cold War. Vietnam acquired particular importance because it was seen as a key to defeating the Soviet Union in the long term. It was believed that maintaining a noncommunist Vietnam was vital to the national interests of the U.S. The fear was that if all of Vietnam became Communist, it would result in the spread of Communism throughout the rest of Southeast Asia. This was called the domino theory, and it was a view with broad support among the political and intellectual leaders of the day.

By the time Kennedy became president in 1961, the U.S. already had one foot in Vietnam. Throughout the 1950s, the U.S. had given billions of dollars of military aid to the French, who were fighting the Communist North Vietnamese for control of the country. The U.S. did not like the idea of helping the French keep control over their foreign territories but hoped it would stop the Communist advance.

Ho Chi Minh

Their hopes didn't come true. The First Indochina War ended with the signing of the Geneva Accords in 1954. The French left and Vietnam split into two separate countries. North Vietnam was led by Ho Chi Minh, a devoted Communist. South Vietnam was led by Ngo Dinh Diem, a passionate anticommunist.

Ngo Dinh Diem

The French were no longer interested in trying to keep a presence in Vietnam. But the U.S. was still very concerned that without a foreign backer, the South Vietnamese government would collapse. By 1961, Communist forces in South Vietnam, called the Vietcong, were making effective gains in the villages and in rural areas. It was clear that if left on its own, noncommunist South Vietnam would not last long.

Kennedy was torn on the issue. When he entered office, former President Eisenhower had warned him specifically about the importance of keeping Southeast Asia from becoming entirely Communist. Kennedy's experience in dealing with the Soviet Union had also led him to be a fierce opponent of Communism. On the other hand,

Kennedy was well aware that the quality of the South Vietnamese leadership was very low, and he was worried that supporting them would be a waste.

Kennedy decided to increase military aid to South Vietnam, giving them huge quantities of military equipment. He also increased the number of so-called "military advisers" sent to Vietnam, U.S. soldiers whose job was to train the South Vietnamese army. In theory, American soldiers were not supposed to engage in combat against Vietcong forces. However, they often did just that. It was one link in the chain of decisions that would ultimately see more than two and a half million Americans serving in Vietnam, of whom more than fifty thousand would never come home alive.

Kennedy's refusal to commit the full weight of American resources to Vietnam would be an issue that would come up again and again, both with Kennedy and later with American policy makers. Kennedy felt pressured by the expectations of the American public. He knew they would punish him politically if Vietnam became Communist. But he also knew they were unwilling to commit fully to war. He remarked privately:

"We don't have a prayer of staying in Vietnam. Those people hate us. . . . But I can't give

up a piece of territory like that to the
Communists and then get the American
people to reelect me."

By 1963, however, it was clear that Kennedy's policies
were not working. The Vietcong were gaining territory in
rural South Vietnam. Moreover, the South Vietnamese
government was in shambles. Ngo Dinh Diem, who had
made himself president after getting rid of the emperor,
was widely hated by his own people. His corruption and the
favoritism he showed to Vietnam's Catholic minority were
extremely unpopular.

Diem's poor leadership had long been a source of concern
for the U.S. Kennedy recognized that Diem's corruption
was losing him support among the Vietnamese. He also
saw that the Vietcong rebels were far more effective
than the South Vietnamese army. Through his advisers,
Kennedy heard rumors that there were forces within the
military seeking to overthrow Diem, but that they needed
American support to do so. Kennedy was unsure what
to do. He knew that Diem was a terrible president, but
he was concerned that his replacement would be even
worse. He also felt that it was inappropriate for the U.S.
to directly engage in the overthrow of an allied head of
state. Ultimately, Kennedy quietly agreed to give support

to the conspiracy against Diem. He expected that Diem would be sent into **exile**. Diem's murder as a result of the conspiracy shocked Kennedy.

ASSASSINATION

On November 22, 1963, while riding in a motorcade in Dallas, Texas, Kennedy was struck down by an assassin's bullet. Shortly after, Lee Harvey Oswald was arrested for the crime. Oswald claimed that he had nothing to do with Kennedy's death and was being framed. A few days later,

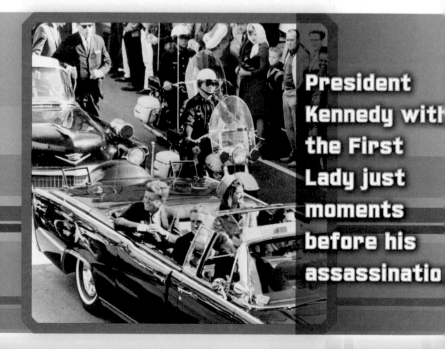

President Kennedy with the First Lady just moments before his assassinatio

Lee Harvey Oswald
after his arrest

before he could be brought to trial, Oswald himself was murdered by a Dallas bartender named Jack Ruby.

Because of the strange circumstances surrounding his death, some Americans continue to believe that Kennedy's murder was the result of a conspiracy. No concrete evidence proving this has ever been found, however, and in 1964 a presidential commission determined that Lee Harvey Oswald had acted alone.

Kennedy's death was met by terrible sadness throughout the country and the world, even by those who did not favor his policies. To this day, many Americans can remember

Kennedy's wife, Jacqueline, and daughter, Caroline, kneel at his grave

exactly where they were and what they were doing when they heard the news of his murder.

Because he died at only forty-six, with so much of his life unfinished, Kennedy is remembered as much for what he did not do as for what he did. His optimism and his vision for the future inspired many Americans. Historians are divided as to whether, if Kennedy had lived longer, the U.S. would have continued their intervention in Vietnam. Shortly before his death, Kennedy had decided to reduce the number of military advisers being provided to South Vietnam. But it also seems possible that the momentum of the conflict would have been impossible to resist, and like the presidents who came after him, Kennedy would have been forced into further military escalation.

HO CHI MINH

HO CHI MINH was a committed leader and a passionate Communist. He served as prime minister and president of North Vietnam and was responsible for many of the war strategies implemented during the Vietnam War.

EARLY LIFE

The man who would later call himself Ho Chi Minh was born Nguyen Sinh Cung, in the year 1890, in a small village in central Vietnam. His father, Nguyen Sinh Sac, had at one point been a government official but quit to become a traveling teacher and healer. He had several sisters and brothers, but they played little role in his life. Family was never very important to Minh. His one overriding goal, throughout his long and extraordinary life, was to free his country from the control of any foreign power.

The Vietnam that Minh was born into was a chaotic place. The French controlled Vietnam, and their presence in the country was a source of anger to many Vietnamese people. Revolts over taxes and French colonial policy were frequent. Minh's father was passionately anti-French, and Minh grew up believing the same. He often fought with his French teachers at school.

After finishing his studies, Minh spent a few months working as a teacher, but he soon grew bored with it and was hired on as a galley boy for a French merchant ship. It would be the beginning of a nearly thirty-year absence from his home country.

Much of this period of Minh's life is a mystery. He never kept a journal, and unlike many public figures, he never told his personal story to a biographer. Although we have a broad outline of his activities during this time, there are many gaps in it.

Minh spent some time traveling throughout Southeast Asia and the Middle East. He then went to the United States, beginning his journey in San Francisco and spending the next year traveling across the country. He was impressed with the fact that American immigrants, of whatever race, were all granted the same legal rights. It was very different from French-run Vietnam, where the Vietnamese did not have legal rights in their own country.

From the U.S., Minh traveled to London. He began to take an interest in politics, investigating the many different types of political beliefs that were popular at that time. For Minh, though, France was the center of the world. After all, it was the French that had invaded his country, and remained in control of it. After spending some time in London, Minh moved to Paris. It was while in Paris that he was introduced to Communism.

Ho Chi Minh in France, 1920

Communism proved to be an extremely popular philosophy,

and soon Communist political parties existed throughout Europe and beyond. At the end of World War I, the Russian Empire collapsed, and was replaced by the Communist Soviet Union. From then on, the Soviet Union became the main sponsor of Communist activities throughout the globe. They placed spies into other governments and gave money and weapons to pro-Communist revolutionaries.

What most attracted Minh to Communism was its opposition to European activities, like the French ruling over Vietnam. Minh joined the Communist party and began writing pro-Communist pamphlets and articles. He became well respected for his intelligence and clever style. But Minh was never a strict believer in Communism. He saw it as the most effective tool for freeing Vietnam from French control. His primary aim was centered on creating a free and independent Vietnam.

Still, Communism was frowned upon by the French government, and Minh's activities gained him attention from the French spy service. In 1924 he moved to Moscow, which had recently become the capital of the Soviet Union. While there, he was trained in Communist policies and made contacts within the Soviet Union. Shortly after, he went to China, where he worked with the Communist forces attempting to gain power there. He also began to organize the large Vietnamese population in China, laying the groundwork for the time when he would return to his homeland. Minh continued to travel throughout the world during this period. He worked as a spy and professional revolutionary. At one point he was arrested in Hong Kong but managed to escape to China. Even though he had not seen his homeland in decades, his reputation as a writer, thinker, and leader of the Vietnamese Communists continued to grow. He developed an almost legendary status within the country of Vietnam itself. The quality of his writings, and his long history as an opponent of French rule, won him many allies.

THE FIRST INDOCHINA WAR

In 1940, the French government in Vietnam was overthrown by the forces of the Japanese Empire. The Japanese portrayed themselves as fellow Asians, rescuing the Vietnamese from unjust French rule. But Minh was not convinced. To support the Japanese against the French, Minh warned, would be to "drive the tiger out the front door while letting the wolf in through the back." His fears would come true. The Japanese were no more interested in giving freedom to the Vietnamese than the French had been.

In early 1941, Minh finally returned to his homeland,

slipping across the border from China. He had spent nearly thirty years in exile and seen dozens of countries around the world. Now it was time to put his experience into practice. In the mountains of northern Vietnam, he met with a small group of committed Communist revolutionaries. There they proclaimed the beginning of the Vietnamese Independence League, which came to be better known as the Vietminh. He also began to use Ho Chi Minh as his official name, which, translated roughly, means "Bringer of Light."

The Vietminh began to launch attacks against the Japanese regime. Military affairs were handled by his brilliant commander, Vo Nguyen Giap. Giap was largely self-taught, and had little in the way of a military education. A high school history teacher turned revolutionary, Giap's pro-Communist activities had caught the attention of the French, and he was forced to flee his home. As revenge, the French had imprisoned and killed his wife, which served

Vo Nguyen Giap

to fuel Giap's desire for revenge. Later, Giap's strategies would be instrumental in overthrowing French rule.

At the time, however, Minh was willing to accept assistance from whoever he thought would be of help in freeing Vietnam. His forces coordinated activities with the Allied forces fighting against the Japanese. The Allies were also happy to provide support to anyone fighting against the Japanese. In 1945, when Minh was deathly sick, a group of U.S. doctors were parachuted in to provide him with medical care, probably saving his life.

By 1945, the U.S. and their allies had all but defeated the Japanese Empire, whose forces were in rapid retreat. Minh and many others hoped that the time had finally come for Vietnam to be an independently governed nation. But the French had other ideas, and they worked to regain their control over Vietnam. At the same time, the Chinese had sent an army into North Vietnam. It looked like China, then run by the anticommunist Chiang Kai-shek, was hoping to gain their own foothold in Vietnam.

Minh decided it would be best to come to an agreement with the French that would allow for the ejection of the Chinese from North Vietnam. When his followers criticized him, he said:

"The last time the Chinese came, they stayed one thousand years. The French are foreigners . . . they are weak. But if the Chinese stay now, they will never go."

This was a classic tool of Minh's, playing one enemy off another to the ultimate benefit of Vietnam. With the help of the French, the Chinese were sent packing.

But peace between the French and the Vietminh was brief. The French government was unwilling to allow the Vietnamese to take meaningful steps toward self-government. For their part, many of the hard-core Vietminh supporters were furious that any accommodation had been made with the French, long their archenemies. Soon, war broke out between the two.

The devastation of Europe after World War II had left the once proud French Republic barely able to pay for their own existence. They needed financial assistance if they hoped to wage military actions in Vietnam, and they turned to the U.S. Initially, the U.S. was skeptical. They had little interest in helping the French continue to maintain control over their colonial possessions. However, they were becoming greatly concerned about the rapid "loss" of Southeast Asia to Communism. President Eisenhower decided to provide the French with billions of dollars in equipment and money to help fund the war in Vietnam.

As it turned out, the worldwide Communist threat that the U.S. feared was nonexistent. Communist China would swiftly become rivals, not allies, with the Soviet Union. Likewise, though the Vietminh were happy to take whatever help they could from the Communist forces, they were always first and foremost concerned with Vietnamese independence. Throughout this period, Minh attempted to come to some sort of an agreement with the U.S. He suggested that a free Vietnam would not take sides in the Cold War. But the U.S. was unwilling to listen, or simply didn't believe him.

The U.S. aid just prolonged the war. The Vietminh quickly revealed themselves to be skilled and excellently led. They could fight effectively with little equipment. They marched for days on end to gain the element of surprise. They were strong in defense and fearless in attack. The French, meanwhile, were troubled by the same difficulties that would later hurt American forces. They were despised by much of the population and they did not understand the local mindset. The French lacked a long-term vision for ending the conflict. They were unable to maintain their hold over the vast jungle territory of Vietnam. Minh at one point compared the conflict to "a grasshopper fighting an elephant," because of the Vietminh's weaknesses in equipment and training. But in this conflict, it would turn out that the grasshopper had advantages the elephant couldn't match.

The Vietminh increased in number and in skill as the war continued. Although at first they were only capable of launching small-scale raids against the French, by 1954 they were able to beat the French in open battle. When the French base at Dien Bien Phu was overrun by Vietminh forces in the spring of 1954, it it would be the final blow. The French wanted out of Vietnam. It was clear that some form of negotiated peace was now critical to ending the war.

THE GENEVA ACCORDS

The Geneva Conference began in April of 1954. Besides the French and the Vietnamese, it also included representatives from Communist China, the Soviet Union, Cambodia, Laos, the U.S., and the United Kingdom. The purpose of it was to find a way to end the ongoing struggle in Vietnam.

Mekong R.

Muong
Phine

NORTH VIET NAM
Cease-Fire Line
July 22, 1954

HUE

THAILAND

L A O S

Tourane

Attopeu

Bassac

Quang
Ngai

Kontum

Pleiku

Cheom
Ksan

Lomphat

Stung
Treng

Song
Cau

CAMBODIA

SOUTH

VIET

NAM

Kompong
Cham

Mekong R.

Phnom
Penh

Mekong R.

Bien Hoa

SAIGON

Phan Thiet

Rach Gia

Mekong R.

South
China Sea

0   100
MILES

AP

South Vietnam and
surrounding countries

The Vietminh hoped for a unified Vietnam under the rule of Ho Chi Minh, or at least a government shared between them and whoever ended up as ruler in South Vietnam. But despite their military successes, the Vietminh position was actually relatively weak. They were forced to rely on the support of China and the Soviet Union, who saw the North Vietnamese as a bargaining chip to be played against the U.S. The U.S. saw the situation in Vietnam as one part of a global struggle against Communism. The French, meanwhile, just wanted to rid themselves of what had become a great burden.

The end result was a confusing muddle of a treaty that provided for immediate peace while virtually guaranteeing future war. Vietnam would be split into two countries. North Vietnam would be a Communist country ruled by Ho Chi Minh and his supporters. South Vietnam would, in theory, be run by Bao Dai, the corrupt former emperor. Bao Dai had little experience as a real leader, having spent most of his life as a pampered elitist. He was not loved by either the North or South Vietnamese. South Vietnam would soon be run entirely by Bao Dai's prime minister, Ngo Dinh Diem. As part of the treaty, the North Vietnamese agreed to retreat from the territory they had conquered in the South. This division was only meant to exist for the short term. A national vote was to be held, the results of which

Vietnamese emperor Bao Dai

would determine whether or not the reunified nation of Vietnam would be run by Ho Chi Minh or the leaders or South Vietnam.

Many Vietminh were furious. They felt that they had lost at the negotiation table what they had won on the battlefield. The Americans, in their minds, were no different from the French, another colonial power to control Vietnam. They hated the South Vietnamese government even more, seeing them as little better than traitors.

Minh was far from pleased by the results, either. In particular, he always deeply regretted the idea of separating Vietnam into two countries. But Ho Chi Minh's greatest political virtue, and the trait that made the Vietminh such a powerful force, was patience. Minh never saw the fight for Vietnam in terms of months or even years. He saw it in terms of decades, a constant, ongoing struggle that would last until a unified Vietnam existed, free of foreign influence. He had succeeded in overturning more than a century of French rule, and in gaining international recognition for North Vietnam. With time, he felt confident he would conquer South Vietnam as well.

Ho Chi Minh's record of governing North Vietnam was mixed. He instituted land reform, which took farmland out of the hands of the small minority of the very wealthy, redistributing it more fairly among the peasants. For this he was widely praised. However, his Communist forces were also responsible for violent "purges" throughout the Vietnamese countryside, imprisoning and killing individuals who had worked for the French, or were simply seen as anticommunist. These kinds of purges were frequently seen whenever a Communist regime took power. They had taken place in the Soviet Union and China. The exact number of dead is unclear, as is the degree to which Minh was directly involved in these mass murders. But they stand out as one of the bloodier and more terrible episodes in the history of North Vietnam. The purges were also politically very foolish. They were the main reasons for the **emigration** of roughly one million North Vietnamese to South Vietnam, most of whom were Catholics who feared the antireligious aspects of Communism.

Ngo Dinh Diem was a corrupt and dishonest leader. After overthrowing the emperor by rigging the local elections, he quickly moved to concentrate political and military power into his hands and the hands of his immediate family. He also refused to hold the nationwide elections called for by the Geneva Accords.

But then, Minh had never assumed that Diem was likely to follow the Geneva Accords, and he did not intend to do the same, either. Although the terms of the Geneva Accords called for the removal of all Vietminh soldiers from South Vietnam, many of them, in fact, stayed. There they quietly worked to strengthen the Communist position, and waited for the time when problems would break out between North and South Vietnam.

Minh was still somewhat hopeful that negotiation was possible with the South Vietnamese government. The two major Communist powers, China and the Soviet Union, were reluctant to involve themselves in a struggle against the United States. Minh worked to play the two against each other, and in 1957 the Soviets agreed to provide arms and training to the Vietminh. Minh now encouraged

President Ho Chi Minh, 1969

those of his soldiers who had stayed in South Vietnam, as well as those South Vietnamese angered by the current government, to begin military operations.

It was the beginning of what would turn into the Vietnam War, but it would not be Minh responsible for fighting it. Sick, aging, and tired, in 1959 Minh stepped down as the Communist Party Leader for North Vietnam, replaced by Le Duan. Though Minh was still held in immensely high regard, he no longer had any immediate political power. He spent the next ten years in the capital city of Hanoi, advising the new government and working to inspire the North Vietnamese.

Statue of
Ho Chi Minh

DEATH AND LEGACY

Having suffered for years from serious health problems,
Ho Chi Minh died on September 2, 1969, in Hanoi. He
did not live to see his dream of a unified Vietnam, but

his actions unquestionably laid the groundwork for its existence. Indeed, it is hard to imagine a single individual more responsible for the birth of modern Vietnam than Ho Chi Minh. For many Vietnamese, "Uncle Ho," as he is called, holds a position of immense respect. Shortly after its capture in 1975, Saigon was renamed Ho Chi Minh City, and his picture is on Vietnamese currency. For others, Minh is thought of much more negatively, as the guiding hand responsible for the violent purges that rocked Vietnam. But even his bitterest enemies could not question the passion that he had to create an independent Vietnam, and the extraordinary struggles he undertook to see his dream become a reality.

LYNDON B. JOHNSON

LYNDON BAINES JOHNSON, vice president to John F. Kennedy, became America's thirty-sixth president after Kennedy's assassination. Although he supported many domestic social programs, his presidential term was best known for the escalation of U.S. involvement in the Vietnam War. He was so exhausted by the war that he declined to run for a second term, becoming the only president in U.S. history to do so.

EARLY LIFE

Lyndon Baines Johnson was born in 1908, in a small farmhouse in Stonewall, Texas. His father, Samuel Ealy Johnson, Jr., was a member of the Texas House of Representatives, as well as a farmer and cattle rancher. His mother, Rebekah Baines, raised the children. Johnson was the eldest child, later followed by three sisters and a brother: Rebekah, Josefa, Sam Houston, and Lucia.

Lyndon B. Johnson at eighteen months old, 1910

Johnson came from an old family, with a long history of political and religious service in the state of Texas. They were not, however, wealthy. Johnson's father lost most of his money in a series of bad investments, and Johnson's upbringing was often difficult. Despite that, he did well in high school, playing baseball and joining the debate team.

In 1926, Johnson borrowed seventy-five dollars and enrolled in the Southwest Texas State Teachers College. To pay for his expenses, he worked odd jobs as a janitor and office helper. While studying to get his degree, Johnson also taught at the Welhausen Mexican School in the South

Texas town of Cotulla. His students were mostly very poor, and working with them gave Johnson an appreciation for their struggles. Of this period in his life, Johnson would later say, "It was then that I made up my mind that this nation could never rest while the door to knowledge remained closed to any American."

In 1930, Johnson graduated from college. He briefly taught debate and public speaking at a high school in Houston but soon found himself drawn into politics. He began working as legislative secretary for Congressman Richard M. Kleberg, a Democrat from Texas. While working for the congressman, he learned valuable lessons about the inner workings of Congress and made important contacts with other politicians and reporters.

It was also at this time that he met Claudia Alta Taylor, better known in history by her nickname, Lady Bird. Set up on a date by a mutual friend, Johnson fell in love immediately, proposing at the end of their first date! Lady Bird was skeptical at first, but finally agreed. They were married ten weeks later, in San Antonio. They had two children, both daughters: Linda, born in 1944, and Luci, born in 1947.

In 1937, Johnson ran for Congress in Texas's tenth district, covering Austin and the surrounding countryside, and won easily. Once in Congress he became a close ally of

Johnson with his wife and two daughters, 1948

the president, Franklin Delano Roosevelt, helping enact his policies. Johnson ran for Senate in 1941 but lost.

When the United States joined World War II in 1941, Johnson became an officer in the U.S. Naval Reserve. In 1942 the president sent Johnson to investigate military conditions in the South Pacific. While in transit between bases, Johnson's plane was fired upon by Japanese fighter aircraft, but the plane escaped unharmed. In recognition of this, Johnson was given the Silver Star, the Navy's third highest medal.

After returning to Washington, Johnson reported the many problems he had seen in the South Pacific to the president. The soldiers were unhappy, he said, and their equipment was not as good as what the Japanese had. Congress elected to make Johnson the head of a sub-committee in charge of fixing some of these problems. Johnson worked hard to try and improve the quality and quantity of naval equipment being provided to the men in the South Pacific.

In 1948, Johnson decided to run for Senate a second time. The election was extremely close, with Johnson ultimately winning by a mere eighty-seven votes! This tiny margin earned him the nickname "Landslide Lyndon." Johnson thought the label was funny, and would use it when he went to Washington.

YEARS IN THE SENATE

Once in the Senate, Johnson gained more power and responsibility. He made friends with important congressional leaders and quickly improved his social standing. In part because of his great effort, Johnson very swiftly rose in the congressional ranks. In 1951, while still serving his first term in the Senate, Johnson was made the Democratic majority whip, which is generally considered the second most powerful position in the Senate. It was an

Johnson supporters in Texas

extraordinary accomplishment for someone so young.

In 1952 the Democratic Party lost their majority in the Senate. Shortly after, Johnson became the Senate minority leader, another very important position. He won his reelection campaign in 1954. In that same year the Democratic Party regained their majority in the Senate, and Johnson became Senate majority leader. In only six years, Johnson had gone from being a little known junior senator to holding the highest office in the Senate. It was an unbelievable rise to power.

It is the job of the majority leader to use the tools of Congress to effectively push forward his or her party's agenda. Even by the standards of the position, Johnson quickly became famous for the control he maintained over the Senate. He developed an incredibly detailed knowledge of all of his fellow senators, their likes and dislikes along with their political views. He knew what to offer people to get them to do what he wanted and was an extremely skilled negotiator. He was also personally an impressive figure, famous for having a very strong presence. If a senator refused to vote the way he wanted him to, Johnson would confront him, intimidating and arguing until his opponent gave in.

In 1955, Johnson suffered a heart attack. He had been a frequent smoker, but he decided to give it up completely and quit smoking for the remainder of his political career.

After twelve years in the Senate, Johnson decided he would run for president in 1960. He waged a close and bitter campaign against John F. Kennedy. Kennedy was chosen to be the Democratic Party's candidate for president during the national convention, and he had twenty-four hours to choose who would run as his vice president. Few expected him to choose Johnson. The primaries had been

Johnson at the
Democratic National
Convention

ugly, and there was personal distrust between the two. But
Kennedy knew that he would need the support of southern
Democrats if he hoped to win the presidency. He hoped
that Johnson, with his deep southern roots, would be able
to help. With Johnson's support, Kennedy was victorious in
the 1960 elections, beating Republican Richard M. Nixon
by an exceptionally slim margin.

VICE PRESIDENT AND BEYOND

Johnson did not enjoy his new position as vice president. The Constitution gives very few specific powers to the position. It is up to the current president to determine what role, if any, his vice president should play. Johnson and Kennedy did not have a close relationship, and the president was unwilling to give Johnson any serious responsibilities. It was a strange position for Johnson, who was previously a powerful and respected congressional leader and now had such a minor role.

Johnson, next to Jackie Kennedy, being sworn in as president after John F. Kennedy's assassination, 1963

All that changed on November 22, 1963, when President Kennedy was tragically struck down by an assassin's bullet. Johnson was sworn in as president and swiftly went about fulfilling his agenda.

Johnson used his early years in office to introduce **liberal** policies that significantly transformed the American landscape. In 1964, Johnson signed the Civil Rights Act into law, overturning almost a century of southern segregationist policies. Johnson was a more active supporter of civil rights than Kennedy had been, even though he knew it would cause him some political trouble. Johnson was also responsible for turning the full powers of the federal government on the Ku Klux Klan, a racist, secretive organization that had been violently resisting integration. In 1967, Johnson nominated Thurgood Marshall to become a Supreme Court justice, the first African American to ever hold the position.

Johnson saw his presidency as an opportunity for government to take an active hand in the improvement of the country. As he put it, "I intend to establish working groups to prepare a series of conferences and meetings—on the cities, on natural beauty, on the quality of education, and on other emerging challenges. From these studies, we will begin to set our course toward the Great Society." These "Great Society" programs included increased

Johnson announcing his nomination of Thurgood Marshall as a Supreme Court justice, 1967

spending on education and health care, job training, government-sponsored housing, and many other government projects. Apart from his policies in Vietnam, Johnson's Great Society programs remain his most enduring, and controversial, legacy. For some, it was an admirable attempt to solve some of society's most deep-rooted problems. For others, it is seen as one of the clearest examples of wasteful and unnecessary government intervention in American history.

Johnson was able to pass so much legislation because of the strong vote of confidence the public had given him in 1964, when he ran for office. Johnson was elected as president with one of the largest margins in history, carrying forty-five states and receiving nearly twice as many votes as his opponent, Barry Goldwater, in the popular election. It seemed Johnson was destined to become one of the most powerful and influential presidents in American history. And yet, amazingly, four years later he refused to run for reelection. He was the only president after World War II to step aside rather than try for a second term. To understand Johnson's reasons for doing so, we need to take a look at what was the defining issue of his presidency: the escalation of the war in Vietnam.

ESCALATION IN VIETNAM

When Johnson became president in 1963, the situation in Vietnam was at a low point. After the assassination of Ngo Dinh Diem, a series of equally incompetent leaders took power, one falling after the other. This quickly reduced the ability of South Vietnam to defend itself from the attacks of the Communist Vietcong. It also convinced many South Vietnamese civilians that they would be better off if the country were run by Ho Chi Minh and his Communist forces. In the countryside, the Vietcong were having marked success. Where earlier they had only been capable of small raids, they were now strong enough to wage open war against the South Vietnamese army, and even to capture cities.

Like Kennedy, Johnson was skeptical of further involvement in Vietnam. He recognized the difficulties in supporting the unpopular South Vietnamese regime. He was also worried that focusing on Vietnam would make it more difficult to fulfill his Great Society programs. However, Johnson refused to be the president history would hold responsible for "losing Vietnam." Years later, he would say of this impossible situation:

"If I left the woman I really loved—the Great Society—in order to get involved . . . (in) a war on the other side of the world, then I would lose everything at home. . . . But if I left that war and let the Communists take over South Vietnam, then I would be seen as a coward and my nation would be seen as an appeaser and we would both find it impossible to accomplish anything for anybody anywhere on the entire globe."

In Johnson's mind, he had no choice but to support the South Vietnamese government, even if that meant sending U.S. troops into battle.

There was one problem—the U.S. Constitution does not give the president authority to declare war. That right is clearly and unarguably given only to Congress. Johnson was unwilling to put his presidential credibility at risk by asking for Congress to approve his sending troops to Vietnam. Johnson needed an incident that would justify direct U.S. involvement in Vietnam to even those members of Congress who were opposed to the war.

That incident would be one of the most debated moments of a long and complicated war. On August 2, 1964, the destroyer USS *Maddox* reported being attacked in the Gulf of Tonkin, a body of water in North Vietnam. In fact, it has never become entirely clear whether or not this event actually happened. It seems more likely that radar images were incorrectly read, suggesting an attack from the North Vietnamese Navy, which did not actually occur. Regardless, it was the opportunity Johnson was looking for. He gave a speech playing up the attacks and insisted that Congress pass the so-called Gulf of Tonkin Resolution. This gave the president authority to send troops into Southeast Asia without a formal declaration of war. In later years, when the cloudy circumstances regarding the Gulf of Tonkin attack became clear to the American public, the resolution was withdrawn.

The Gulf of Tonkin incident would become one of the turning points in the war. Before it, the U.S. provided advice and assistance to the South Vietnamese army, and flew bombing runs against Vietcong positions. Afterward, Johnson began to send hundreds of thousands of American soldiers to South Vietnam, which reshaped the very nature of the country. Saigon was filled with American servicemen. Billions of dollars in development aid were sent to Vietnam. Harbors had to be built to accommodate U.S. ships and airstrips for U.S. planes to fly into.

All of this was overseen by General William Westmoreland, whom Johnson chose to oversee this new phase of the war in Vietnam. At first, the troops stabilized the situation. The U.S. military, better trained and with better equipment, reversed the successes of the Communist Vietcong, pushing them farther north. However, this cost many U.S. lives. By the end of 1964, there were 184,000 American servicemen in Vietnam. By the end of 1968, 537,000 Americans were fighting in Indochina.

Still, things seemed to be improving. After the overthrow and death of Ngo Dinh Diem, South Vietnam suffered from constant changes in leadership. In 1967, however, Nguyen Cao Ky took office as prime minister. Though not much more competent or less corrupt than the men who had held the office before him, he was at least powerful enough to remain in control of the country for several years. This provided the U.S. with a semi-stable partner.

Public feeling over the war was deeply mixed, and remains so to this day. Many Americans were actively against having any military presence in Vietnam. Young people in America were particularly opposed, and they began to object to it with marches, sit-ins, and other forms of mostly nonviolent public protests. However some people believed that, if America was going to be sending soldiers into Vietnam, then the nation needed to be a hundred percent committed to success, rather than continue gradually escalating the conflict. Between the

Anti-Vietnam War protesters

two groups, Johnson's support began to decline. Johnson was very aware of the conflicting feelings regarding the Vietnam War. He actively worked to downplay the United States' involvement. He rarely gave press conferences on the subject, and didn't hold any rallies in support of his Vietnam policy.

Johnson was also conscious of the horrors ongoing in Vietnam and desperately wanted to find a way to end the war without bringing shame to America. But Ho Chi Minh and the Vietcong were unwilling to compromise. Though their losses were far greater than those suffered by the U.S., they remained committed to the fight.

In a letter, Minh wrote that if the Americans "want to make war for twenty years then we shall make war for twenty years. If they want to make peace, we shall make peace and invite them to afternoon tea."

Ho Chi Minh was unwilling to accept any sort of agreement that allowed the U.S. to continue to support the South Vietnamese government. The U.S. knew that without their backing, South Vietnam would soon fall. The situation seemed unresolvable.

By 1968, four years after Johnson had first sent troops to

Vietnam, the situation was at a standstill, and Americans were getting fed up with the lack of progress. General Westmoreland continued making optimistic, perhaps even inaccurate, statements suggesting that the war was being fought successfully and would soon be over. At the same time, Westmoreland called for more American soldiers to be sent to Vietnam each year through a military draft.

In late January 1968, the Vietcong violated a cease-fire planned for the Vietnamese New Year (also known as the Tet Festival) and launched a massive attack against the U.S. and the South Vietnamese army. In military terms,

Johnson at his ranch, 1964

the Tet Offensive was a defeat for the Vietcong, who suffered far more casualties than they caused. But it came at a time when Johnson's administration was insisting that the Vietcong were all but defeated. The simple fact that the Vietcong were capable of staging such a large attack showed that Johnson's claims were false.

LATER LIFE

By 1968, Johnson was exhausted. His inability to find a way out of Vietnam, along with the increasingly bitter divide in public opinion, were more than he was willing to handle for another four years. He unexpectedly announced that he would not run for president in 1968. In a three-way race, Republican former Vice President Richard Nixon defeated Hubert Humphrey, Johnson's replacement, as well as George Wallace, a noted racist.

After leaving office, Johnson returned to his ranch in Stonewall, Texas. He worked on his memoirs and spent time with his family but had no further direct involvement in national politics. He suffered another heart attack in 1972, which largely debilitated him. On January 22, 1973, at the age of sixty-four, he suffered a third heart attack, from which he did not survive.

Johnson wanted to be remembered, first and foremost, for his attempt to turn America into a Great Society and for his significant contributions to civil rights. But history remembers him, for better or worse, as the man most responsible for the escalation of the conflict in Vietnam, and for the consequences of that decision.

WILLIAM WESTMORELAND

WILLIAM WESTMORELAND was a United States Army general and was appointed Chief of the General Staff from 1968–1972. He commanded military operations during the height of the Vietnam War. His military decisions were seen as controversial, but his commitment to the Vietnam War remains unquestioned.

EARLY LIFE

William Childs Westmoreland was born in Spartanburg County, South Carolina, on March 26, 1914, to Eugenia Talley Childs and James Ripley Westmoreland. His father was a wealthy banker and merchant, and his early home life was comfortable. He was a devoted member of the Boy Scouts of America, reaching the highest rank, Eagle Scout, at the early age of fifteen.

After completing high school, he went on to college at the Citadel, a private military school. After one year, however, Westmoreland transferred to West Point. Although his grades were mediocre, upon graduation he received the coveted Pershing Sword, the award given to the most able cadet at the academy. Afterward he was assigned to Fort Sill, Oklahoma. While there he would meet Katherine Van Deusen, the daughter of another officer. Later, in 1947, they would marry, and ultimately have three children: a daughter,

Westmoreland with his wife and family

Katherine Stevens Westmoreland; a son, James Ripley Westmoreland II; and another daughter, Margaret Childs Westmoreland.

When the U.S. entered World War II in 1941, Westmoreland moved up quickly through the ranks, becoming a lieutenant colonel. He was given command of the 34th Field Artillery Battalion and fought in Sicily and North Africa. In 1944, when the Allied forces invaded France, the 34th Field Artillery Battalion fought so effectively that Westmoreland was made a colonel. He was decorated for his actions in a battle at the Rhine, where despite coming under heavy enemy fire, he remained unhurt. Of the battle he would write, "Somehow none of the enemy's shells had my number." By the end of World War II he had been made head of the 60th Infantry. Later, he was asked to take command of the 504th Parachute Infantry Regiment.

Westmoreland was one of the army's rising stars. He had gained a reputation as an excellent leader with a forward-thinking point of view. He was also famous for the care and attention he paid to his men, with whom he was popular. In 1950 he became an instructor at the Command and General Staff College, then later at the U.S. Army War College itself. In 1952, with the Korean War raging, Westmoreland was given command of the 187th Regimental Combat Team. He oversaw their operations in Korea for a year then returned to the U.S. He was made secretary of the Army General Staff in 1955, and three years later, he took command of the famous 101st Airborne Division in Fort Campbell, Kentucky. In 1960 he would become superintendent of West Point, taking over the

Westmoreland as superintendent of West Point, 1960

school he had graduated from nearly thirty years before.

TAKING CONTROL IN VIETNAM

After the Gulf of Tonkin incident in August of 1964, President Johnson received congressional approval to send U.S. soldiers to Vietnam. To lead them, he turned to Westmoreland, whose broad range of experience and enthusiastic attitude made him seem like the perfect fit for such a position. Westmoreland took over Military Assistance Command, Vietnam—the task force responsible for running military policy in Vietnam.

Westmoreland had one simple goal: win the war. After

years of half measures, the U.S. was making a full commitment to ensuring the safety of South Vietnam. By the end of 1965, 184,000 soldiers were serving beneath him in Vietnam, accompanied by many billions of dollars in equipment and aid.

The problem was, of course, that no one knew exactly how to go about defeating the Vietminh. The war in Vietnam was a nontraditional war, very different from those the U.S. had fought in Korea or during World War II. In traditional conflicts, an army attempts to conquer and occupy the enemy's territory, gradually pushing them

Westmorelan speaking to helicopter troops in South Vietnam, 1964

farther and farther back, capturing their troops and equipment. But the Vietcong did not seek to capture or hold territory. They fought what is called a **guerrilla war**, striking at U.S. weaknesses and refusing to offer a clear target for U.S. warplanes and artillery.

Hidden throughout the vast jungles of Vietnam, often in hidden underground

A tunnel in South Vietnam

tunnels, the Vietcong were hard to find and impossible to bring into open battle. They avoided large-scale conflict, attacking unexpectedly, then fading away just as quickly. They laid deadly booby traps, from the newest Soviet land mines to old-fashioned poison pit traps. The Vietcong and Vietminh were masters at this style of warfare, having perfected their abilities against the French during the long and brutal First Indochina War. The U.S., by contrast, had very little experience with this type of combat and suffered because of it.

There were other ways in which the Vietnam conflict did not resemble traditional war. The inability to distinguish between the enemy and Vietnamese civilians was one of the great horrors of the conflict. The Vietcong would often infiltrate themselves among Vietnamese civilians, then attack U.S. soldiers. The Vietcong knew that any civilian casualties caused by the U.S. would serve as effective recruiting tools, and did not hesitate to put their fellow countrymen in danger. It presented a nightmarish situation for U.S. troops. Either they would allow themselves to be fired upon by the enemy, or risk killing innocent civilians.

As the war continued, U.S. soldiers found themselves the victims of attacks while they were off duty, or by Vietcong spies pretending to be noncombatants. In Vietnam, there was no clear "front," a military term which means the line of contact between allied forces and the enemy. For the U.S. soldier in Vietnam, death could come anywhere and at any time. One could step on a land mine while walking through the jungle, or be ambushed by a squad of Vietcong while on patrol. A soldier might find himself victim of a terrorist bomb while getting a drink at a bar in Saigon, or shot by a sniper while on base.

By the mid-sixties the average U.S. soldier was increasingly likely to have been drafted into the army, rather than to have volunteered. This provided much of the inspiration for the antiwar movement, as many thousands of American men found themselves forced to fight in a conflict which they didn't believe in. Refusing to serve was illegal, and meant jail time for any "draft dodger." Draftees were signed to year-long "tours," twelve months spent within the war zone of Vietnam. This was also a modification from earlier conflicts, and one that many top military leaders disliked. A year was not enough time, they argued, for a soldier to gain enough experience to fight effectively in Vietnam. By the time he had learned everything he

Veterans protesting the Vietnam War

needed to know, he was sent back home, replaced by a less-skilled recruit. This system made for a particularly bitter experience of war, one that was very different from that experienced by the men who fought in World War II and the Korean War.

Westmoreland recognized the problems, but he believed he saw a way forward for the U.S. Westmoreland's strategy was relatively simple. He knew that America's superior firepower, in particular their powerful air force, could be used to devestate the Vietcong. The only problem was that the Vietcong knew this as well, and therefore were generally unwilling to put themselves in situations where the U.S. could use their heavy bombers. Westmoreland decided that the new U.S. policy was to actively seek out and destroy the Vietcong. From now on, success would be measured by the number of enemy killed. U.S. soldiers would sweep through enemy territory. They would seek out the Vietcong, pin them down, then call for air support to fire.

More generally, Westmoreland argued that the U.S. needed to follow a policy of attrition, a military strategy in which one side attempts to wear down their opponent by wounding or killing enemy combatants. The focus of the U.S. was to locate and destroy the Vietcong. Because the U.S. was more effective in killing the Vietcong, Westmoreland believed that eventually the North

A B-52 plane unloading bombs on enemy territory in South Vietnam

Vietnamese government would be forced to negotiate for peace. So long as the U.S. remained committed, he thought victory was certain. In 1967, he told Congress:

> "It is evident to me that (the enemy) believes our Achilles heel is our resolve . . . Your continued strong support is vital to the success of our mission . . . Backed at home by resolve, confidence, patience, determination, and continued support, we will prevail in Vietnam over the Communist aggressor!"

Westmoreland
speaking to
Congress

And at first, Westmoreland's strategy seemed effective. Before the introduction of U.S. troops, the Vietcong were closing in on Saigon and controlled much of South Vietnam. By 1966, two years after Westmoreland had been put in control of the war effort, these gains had been reversed. For all of their experience and skill, the Vietcong had yet to face an enemy as powerful as the U.S. military. Westmoreland had also developed several new tactics that were used successfully against the Vietcong. Often, attack helicopters were used to ferry U.S. soldiers into combat zones, dropping them off, providing air support, then returning them to base after the battle was over. The U.S. also stepped up the intensity of their bombing campaign. Waves of B-52 bombers dropped thousands of tons of explosives on North and South Vietnam. Taken together, these new developments meant that the U.S. was causing more casualties than they were suffering. According to Westmoreland's strategy of attrition, the U.S. was winning the war.

However, these military successes had brought the U.S. no closer to victory. The Vietcong and their sponsors in North Vietnam did not see the conflict in the same terms as Westmoreland. The defeats they suffered against the U.S. were setbacks, nothing more. They regrouped and resupplied, and showed up to fight again. The Communist Chinese were able to replace the equipment that the U.S. destroyed, and the North Vietnamese themselves seemed endlessly willing to provide more manpower to replace the casualties suffered at the hands of the U.S.

The Vietcong also proved to be a skilled and flexible enemy. The U.S. Army required huge and expensive amounts of equipment to function effectively. But the Vietcong were able to survive with the tiny trickle of supplies sent down to them through the mountains of North Vietnam. Much of

them were ferried along what was called the Ho Chi Minh
Trail, a series of tiny, winding pathways that stretched
through Cambodia, a country next to Vietnam. Communist
forces would march hundreds of miles, across mountains
and through jungles, carrying supplies on their backs.
Moreover, despite the terrible losses they were suffering,
the Vietcong were still capable of reinforcing themselves
at a far faster rate than the U.S. was willing to commit
troops. By the end of 1965, Communist forces were putting
twice as many men into combat as the U.S.

In public, Westmoreland was always optimistic about the
war. In private, he was asking the president to send more
troops, while expressing a recognition that expanding the
number of U.S. troops in the region would not immediately
lead to victory. Johnson again found himself in an
impossible position. Having already committed U.S. forces
to the conflict, he felt that to remove them without a clear
victory would be interpreted as cowardly, with devastating
consequences both for his own political career and for the
future of the Cold War. But the Vietcong's ability to find
new reinforcements was not affected by U.S. military
activity, while there were practical limits to the number of
men that Johnson could commit to the conflict.

Westmoreland was unhappy at the restrictions placed
upon U.S. military activity by President Johnson. Though

the North Victnamese were openly providing supplies and manpower to the Vietcong, operations within North Vietnam were forbidden. As mentioned, the North Vietnamese often sent equipment and reinforcements through trails running through the neighboring countries of Cambodia and Laos, neither of which the U.S. could attack. Westmoreland argued for expanding the conflict into Cambodia and Laos, as well as considering open attacks against North Vietnam. There were practical political reasons why these options were impossible. But these restrictions seemed to suggest that the U.S. was somehow not "serious" about winning the war in Vietnam, a belief many Americans still hold today.

THE TET OFFENSIVE

In 1968, the Vietcong and their North Vietnamese allies broke a cease-fire celebrating the Vietnamese New Year and launched a massive attack. It was called the Tet Offensive, and it would be the turning point of the war.

The Tet Offensive was a direct attack on American and allied South Vietnamese positions. In military terms, it was a disaster for the Vietcong forces. Tens of thousands of Vietcong soldiers died, with the U.S. and South Vietnamese forces losing relatively few men in comparison. In fact, the Tet Offensive violated the usual strategy of the Vietcong. It

President Johnson and
General Westmoreland

was a straightforward offensive, rather than the guerilla-style warfare they had mastered. In a straight-up fight with the U.S. and South Vietnamese Army, without the benefit of tanks, heavy guns, or air support, the Vietcong were massacred.

But strangely, and despite the horrible casualties suffered by the Vietcong, the Tet Offensive achieved its purpose. It showed the American people that the war in Vietnam was far from being over, that the Vietcong were not beaten. The fact that the Vietcong were capable of attempting and launching the Tet Offensive after years of fighting with the U.S. was evidence that the strategy the U.S. had adopted was not effective in reducing the Vietcong's ability to make war. Shortly after the Tet Offensive, Westmoreland all but admitted as much when he asked President Johnson to add another 200,000 soldiers to the 500,000 that were already serving under his command. When this news was leaked to the American public, it sparked outrage.

More than this, the Tet Offensive suggested to many Americans that President Johnson and General Westmoreland could not be trusted to provide accurate information about the war. The optimistic predictions that

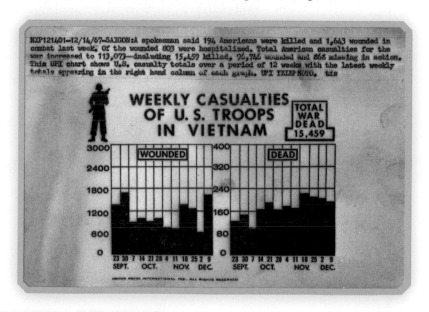

the American people had been hearing for several years seemed to be clearly false. Many historians point to the Tet Offensive as being the moment when the American public turned against the war. During a television broadcast at that time, beloved newsman Walter Cronkite said, "[W]e are mired in a stalemate . . . the only rational way out then will be to negotiate, not as victors." He seemed to be speaking for many Americans in saying so. After hearing it, President Johnson was said to have remarked, "If I've lost Cronkite, I've lost Middle America."

Walter Cronkite

The Tet Offensive had proved Westmoreland's strategy was ineffective. It was clear a change was necessary, but firing him would have been a political impossibility. He was made Chief of the General Staff of the United States Army. He was replaced in Vietnam by General Creighton William Abrams, Jr.

Westmoreland's strategy of attrition was fundamentally based on misguided principles, and a lack of understanding of the mindset of the Communist Vietnamese. But in this he was hardly alone; virtually every American military and political leader engaged in the Vietnam conflict found themselves equally incapable of understanding the enemy. In fact, from a purely military perspective, Westmoreland's strategy was logical, even effective. It was responsible for a greater number of Vietcong and Vietminh deaths than American.

But wars have both political and military aspects. Westmoreland's success on the battlefield never did anything to affect the political issues at hand. The South Vietnamese government was always weak and incapable of standing without U.S. assistance. The Vietcong and their supporters in North Vietnam were unwilling to compromise. They felt that any number of casualties was an acceptable sacrifice if it meant their ultimately assuming control over an undivided Vietnam. By contrast, neither the American people, nor their leaders, were ever willing to make such sacrifices.

What Westmoreland did not appreciate was that the Vietcong were willing to accept far greater casualties than were the U.S. forces. As Ho Chi Minh had told his French adversaries many years before, "You can kill ten of our men for every one we kill of yours. But even at those odds, you will lose and we will win." In fact, the ratio would be closer to twenty, but Minh's arithmetic would still hold true. Estimates of total casualties among the Vietcong and their North Vietnamese supporters are still much disputed, but

Military troops at Westmoreland's funeral ceremony at West Point, 2005

it is almost certainly over a million. By contrast, the U.S. suffered a comparatively small fifty thousand dead. But in the end, as Minh predicted, it would be the U.S. that left.

LATER LIFE

Westmoreland remained Chief of the General Staff of the United States Army until 1972, when he retired from active service in the military. He oversaw the shift from an army dominated by draftees to the current all-volunteer force. In 1982 he sued CBS News over an interview in which he was accused of deliberately misrepresenting the number of Vietcong soldiers during his years in command of U.S. forces in Vietnam. While the case was still on trial, CBS agreed to issue an official apology and Westmoreland withdrew the suit.

Westmoreland would argue for the strategic importance of the Vietnam conflict for the rest of his life. For him it was a necessary conflict, one that had a purpose even though the U.S. did not emerge victorious. At one point he wrote, "By virtue of Vietnam, the U.S. held the line for ten years and stopped the dominoes from falling." Westmoreland died on July 18, 2005, at the age of ninety-one, in Charleston, South Carolina. Though respected for his lifetime of service, many historians identify his strategy in Vietnam as misguided and ineffective.

HENRY KISSINGER

HENRY KISSINGER was a German-born American writer, political scientist, national security advisor, and Nobel Peace Prize winner. He served as the U.S. secretary of state under presidents Nixon and Ford. He negotiated the Paris Peace Accords, which ended American involvement in the Vietnam War. He is known as an incredibly important and influential political leader.

EARLY LIFE

Henry Kissinger was born Heinz Alfred Kissinger in 1923 in the town of Fürth, in Bavaria, Germany. His father, Louis, was a schoolteacher. His mother, Paula Stern Kissinger, was a homemaker. He had one brother, named Walter. Kissinger and his family were Jewish, and as Adolf Hitler's **Nazi** regime rose to power, they realized Germany was no longer safe for them. In 1938 they moved to the United States, moving to New York City. Kissinger would spend his teenage years in northern Manhattan, in the large community of German Jews living there. Like most immigrants of the time, Kissinger's family was poor. He worked in a factory making shaving brushes to help make ends meet.

After graduating from high school, Kissinger began taking classes in accounting at the City College of New York. However, his schooling was interrupted by the outbreak of World War II, when he was drafted into the U.S. Army. Kissinger served in the 84th Infantry Division, seeing combat in France and

Kissinger at age eleven with his brother, Walter

Germany. After the war officially ended, Kissinger worked for army intelligence, overseeing a German territory that was then controlled by the U.S.

In 1946 Kissinger returned to the U.S. He enrolled at Harvard University, seeking a degree in political science. He was an exceptionally talented student, graduating in 1950 with highest honors. In 1954 he received his doctorate from Harvard. After completing his doctoral program he remained on at Harvard as a professor. But Kissinger's ultimate aim was to be in a position where he was making policy, not just discussing it. It wasn't long before he left Harvard for Washington.

When President Johnson declined to run for reelection in 1968, the Democrats were left scrambling for an alternative. Torn between pro-war and antiwar factions, the Democrats nominated Hubert Humphrey. His opponent was Richard M. Nixon. Nixon, a Republican whose political career seemed over after losing the presidency to John F. Kennedy in 1960, had returned to the political scene. While portraying the entry into Vietnam as the fault of the previous two administrations, both Democratic, he also promised voters that he had a "secret plan" to win the war in Vietnam. Voters were happy to believe him, and he defeated Humphrey to become president.

The problem, unfortunately, was that Nixon had no secret

plan to win the war in Vietnam. What he did have was Henry Kissinger, who would quickly become Nixon's chief foreign policy aide, first as national security adviser, then as secretary of state. Kissinger had acquired a reputation as a brilliant politician and a genius planner. He preferred to work in secrecy, never showing all of his cards. Though fluent in English, he still had a German accent, and his curious and distinct way of talking became something of a

Kissinger being sworn in as secretary of state, with President Nixon, 1973

trademark. Indeed, Kissinger managed to achieve a level of celebrity status that was rare among individuals in his position. He attended film premieres and was photographed with starlets on his arm. But this was all a cover for his extraordinary commitment to politics.

By 1969, the Vietnam War had reached a period of bloody standstill. General Westmoreland had been replaced in July 1968 with General Creighton Abrams, Jr., who had begun to institute Nixon's new policy of "Vietnamization." This was an attempt by the U.S. to shift more military duties onto the army of South Vietnam. A greater emphasis was placed on training the South Vietnamese to fight for themselves, with the U.S. playing a supporting role. The hope was that the U.S. would continue to provide equipment for the South Vietnamese, as well as using their air force in support of South Vietnamese troops. The decrease in U.S. forces would also allow Nixon to uphold one of his major campaign promises, which was that he would end the draft, switching to the all-volunteer army that we have today.

Kissinger and Nixon both saw Vietnam as an unfortunate distraction from the Cold War. In contrast to Presidents Kennedy and Johnson, who saw the U.S. and the Soviet Union as permanent and bitter enemies, Kissinger believed that cooperation between the two was both necessary and possible. Kissinger wished to improve the relationship

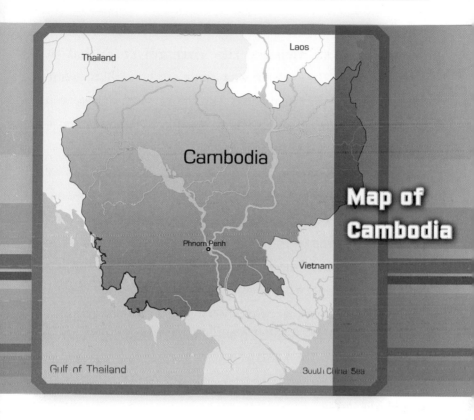

Map of Cambodia

between the U.S. and the Soviet Union. He envisioned a situation he called detente, in which both sides recognized the other as a rightful world power with certain foreign interests, rather than enemies to be confronted.

For any of that to be possible, however, the U.S. needed to leave Vietnam, and to do so in a way that left their national pride intact. "Peace with honor" was the new motto, but it was easier said than done. The problem facing Kissinger was the same problem that had faced President Johnson and his team of advisers. The Vietminh knew that they were winning the war. It was clear that the U.S. wanted out of Vietnam. Without them, the South Vietnamese would be unable to maintain the fight. In short, time was on the side of the Vietcong, and they knew it.

Nixon and Kissinger recognized that the Vietminh were in a better bargaining position. They knew they needed to do something to reshape the situation. Nixon and Kissinger decided that the U.S. needed to raise the stakes. They hoped to convince the Vietminh that if they did not come to an agreement with Nixon at the bargaining table, he would turn the full force of the American military against the Vietminh, escalating the conflict to an intensity the Vietminh could not match. Nixon called it his "Madman Theory," saying:

"I want the North Vietnamese to believe I've reached the point where I might do *anything* to stop the war. We'll just slip the word to them that, 'for God's sake, you know Nixon is obsessed about Communism. We can't restrain him when he's angry—and he has his hand on the nuclear button.'"

But for the Madman Theory to work, the U.S. needed a new threat. Nixon decided to authorize a series of secret bombings in Cambodia. Cambodia is a country next to Vietnam. The Ho Chi Minh Trail, the route by which the Vietminh resupplied their forces in the South, ran through Cambodia. Nixon and Kissinger believed that by bombing the trail, they would both injure the ability of the Vietminh to continue the war and show the leadership of North Vietnam that they were serious. The problem, of course,

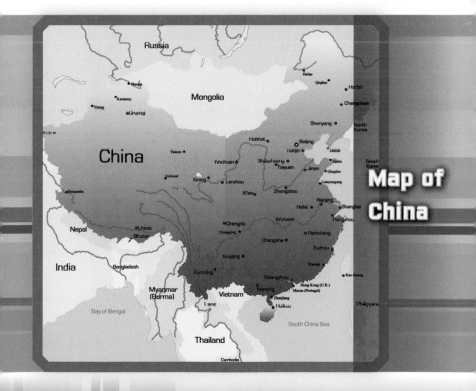

Map of China

was that Cambodia was a neutral country and could not be legally bombed. When the American public discovered the bombings four years later, it caused an uproar among the already passionate antiwar movement. To this day, it remains an immensely controversial act, one that many still criticize Kissinger for.

NIXON GOES TO CHINA

Meanwhile, Kissinger was quietly laying the groundwork for what would be one of the most important **geopolitical** shifts of the twentieth century. Although mainland China had been a Communist country for almost twenty years, the U.S. refused to grant them official recognition. Technically, as far as the U.S. was concerned, the legitimate government of China was still that of the anticommunist leader Chiang Kai-shek. But he and his forces had been ejected from the mainland in 1949 and, in fact, only held control over the small island nation of Taiwan. The U.S. refusal to maintain official relations with a country the size and importance of China was crazy, but seemingly impossible to fix.

Kissinger saw within this thorny problem the seeds of a great opportunity to weaken the Soviet Union. In theory, Communism was meant to be a philosophy that outweighed national concerns, with everyone working together to advance the Communist agenda. In reality, this was not the case at all. The Soviet Union saw China as a territory that ought to follow its orders. The Chinese, needless to say, had no interest in seeing their foreign policy run by another country, even if that country was a Communist one. By the late sixties, the Chinese and the Soviets were bitter rivals.

If Kissinger could further split apart the two largest Communist nations, it would strengthen the U.S. Furthermore, as Communist China had long been the main supporter of the Vietminh and Vietcong, better relations between the U.S. and China might provide the opportunity for the U.S. to weaken their enemies in Vietnam. China was equally interested in creating a relationship with the U.S., recognizing them as a potential ally against the Soviet Union.

Kissinger was far from the first person to recognize the value of building a relationship with Communist China. Previous presidents, however, had been fearful of taking such a dramatic step, thinking that they might lose domestic support if they seemed "soft" on the Communist threat. Nixon had more than proved himself as an anticommunist, so he could afford to make an agreement with China.

Between 1969 and 1971, Kissinger made two visits to China, the first one top secret. There he met with important Chinese officials, working to smooth over areas of concern and bring the two nations closer to agreement. Kissinger's meetings paved the way for official recognition of China by the U.S. On July 15, 1971, it was announced to a stunned public that Nixon would pay an official visit to China. This was a step toward recognition that Communist China was the official and legitimate government of China. Nixon's famous visit to the country in February 1972 is recognized as a milestone in U.S. history, and one of the great accomplishments of the Nixon administration and for Henry Kissinger.

The results of the improvement in relations between China and the U.S. were monumental. Though the U.S. and China never became formal allies, they were no longer in a state of conflict. Indeed, it became clear that there were many areas of possible cooperation between the two countries. In particular, the U.S. and China formed an unofficial alliance against the Soviet Union. The Soviets, recognizing this development and frightened of it, were themselves more willing to cooperate with the U.S.

THE U.S. LEAVES VIETNAM

The North Vietnamese were quick to recognize they may be in trouble. Improved relations between the U.S. and China threatened to isolate them from their main supporter.

President Nixon shaking hands with Chinese Communist leader Mao Zedong in China, 1972

As part of their improved relations with the U.S., China became less willing to provide the North Vietnamese with the equipment and support they needed to continue fighting. The Vietminh adopted two solutions to this problem. First, they turned increasingly toward the Soviet Union as a new source of support. In the later days of the war, the vast majority of their arms and ammunition began to come from the Soviets rather than the Chinese. Second, the Vietminh became open to finding some sort of diplomatic solution that would allow the U.S. to leave Vietnam.

Negotiations between the U.S. and North Vietnam had been attempted since the Johnson administration, without success. North Vietnam insisted that the U.S. remove the South Vietnamese president, Nguyen Van Thieu, from power and replace him with someone more acceptable to the Communist leadership. Nixon was unwilling to do this, and so the negotiations went nowhere.

By 1972, however, the situation had changed. The war was beginning to turn against the North Vietnamese. Their largest attack of that year, called the "Easter Offensive," had been a failure. The U.S. had improved its relationship with China and was working to do the same with the Soviet Union. It seemed possible that both of the two great Communist powers might turn against the North Vietnamese, a potential catastrophe. In a series of secret meetings between Henry Kissinger and his North Vietnamese counterpart, Le Duc Tho, an agreement was reached. The leadership in Hanoi agreed to withdraw their demands for Nguyen Van Thieu's removal. A cease-fire between the North and South Vietnamese was to be scheduled. The government of South Vietnam was to be determined by peaceful negotiations between the government in Saigon and the Vietcong. Prisoners of war were to be sent back to their home countries. Kissinger held a press conference announcing that "peace is at hand."

Kissinger with North Vietnamese negotiators in Paris

There was only one problem: The South Vietnamese government did not accept the terms of the treaty. They feared, rightly as it turned out, that without the U.S. to support them, their military position would collapse. Nguyen Van Thieu went on the radio and attacked the terms of the treaty, misrepresenting them to the South Vietnamese public. In turn, the North Vietnamese became equally furious. It seemed to them that Kissinger had been playing a double game and had negotiated dishonestly.

Kissinger speaking with President Nixon after retuning from the Paris peace talks

Kissinger worked to convince the South Vietnamese that the cease-fire was in their best interests. Nixon promised the South Vietnamese that the U.S. would continue to support them with equipment and, if necessary, by continued bombing of the North Vietnamese. To convince President Thieu of his seriousness, Nixon authorized a massive bombing campaign, called "Operation Linebacker." Operation Linebacker was also meant to remind the North Vietnamese of what the U.S. was capable of if they chose to stop negotiating. It was a very curious sort of peace treaty, which required an increased level of violence to achieve it. Finally, Kissinger managed to convince President Thieu that if he did not agree to the terms of the cease-fire, the U.S. would withdraw their support of South Vietnam. Without any other option, Thieu agreed to sign.

Both the North and South Vietnamese badly broke the terms of the cease-fire. No real peace was reached in Vietnam, but it provided a cover by which the U.S. could exit the conflict without seeming to have been beaten. "Peace with honor" had been achieved. In 1973, in recognition of his work to achieve a cease-fire in Vietnam, the Nobel Prize committee elected to award both Kissinger and Tho the peace prize. Tho declined to accept the award, saying that peace had yet to be truly achieved. Kissinger accepted it, however.

The Paris Peace Accords were meant to provide the government of South Vietnam with the opportunity to stand on their own. Their terms allowed the U.S. to continue to replace military equipment and ammunition so long as the fighting continued, and to provide support for the South Vietnamese army. The North Vietnamese believed that the terms of the cease-fire were to their advantage. Without the full might of the U.S. military, they were sure of a swift victory over the South Vietnamese. In fact, Nixon's policy

Kissinger with President Nixon in the Oval Office after his Nobel Peace Prize nomination

of Vietnamization had resulted in a dramatic improvement in the fighting qualities of the South Vietnamese. With Nixon's promise to further support the South Vietnamese with bombing strikes if Saigon became endangered, it seemed that South Vietnam would hold out against the North.

By 1974, however, the political scene within the U.S. had drammatically changed. President Nixon had resigned the office of president. He had been implicated in what would become known as the Watergate scandal. Put simply, members of Nixon's staff broke into the Democratic Party headquarters in an effort to sabotage their operations. Nixon worked to cover up the crime. When his actions were discovered, he resigned rather than face impeachment, the process by which Congress removes the president from office.

It was a shock and a humiliation to the country, and in the congressional elections an angry nation voted in a Democratic majority. The Democrats and much of the country were sick of the war and no longer willing to support the South Vietnamese government. Even before Nixon's resignation, Congress had turned firmly against the war. In 1973 the Senate passed the Case-Church Amendment, which denied funding for all further U.S. military activity in Vietnam. Without the continued support of the U.S., the South Vietnamese were unable to hold on to the territory they had won. The North Vietnamese launched a massive attack in the spring of 1975. The South Vietnamese regime collapsed, and on April 30, 1975, Communist forces entered Saigon.

This remains an intensely debated issue to this day. For

individuals who supported the war, America's refusal to back its allies in South Vietnam was a terrible betrayal. For those who believed the war was a mistake, it was a decision far too long in coming.

By then, America had increasingly shifted the focus of its foreign policy toward different regions of the world. In that sense, Kissinger's policy had been successful. Though the South Vietnamese were defeated by the North, it did not significantly affect the balance of power between the U.S. and the Soviet Union. Indeed, in the long term, the improved relationship between the U.S. and China did more to turn the tide of the Cold War than the fall of South Vietnam.

LATER LIFE

So great was Kissinger's reputation that even after Nixon resigned his office, the next president, Gerald R. Ford, decided to keep his services as secretary of state. Indeed, few individuals in the history of the country can be said to have had such a long and critical role in developing U.S. foreign policy.

In 1977, Kissinger left the government and returned to academia. He continues to be one of the most respected individuals in the field of foreign policy. His books on the subject are bestsellers, and presidents and leaders continue to ask for his advice. At the same time, many of his actions remain deeply controversial, in particular his support of the secret bombings in Cambodia. What is inarguable, however, is that he played a key role in ending the Vietnam conflict.

CONCLUSION

In 1973, with a cease-fire in place, the U.S. began to remove their combat troops from Vietnam. A small number of support troops remained, to provide training and coordinate with the army of South Vietnam. The South Vietnamese military fought far better than was expected, but against the might of the Vietcong, supported by the North Vietnamese and their Soviet backers, they steadily lost territory.

Still, by 1975 very few people thought that the nation of South Vietnam was in danger. The U.S. believed that Saigon would hold out for at least another year. But a massive attack launched in March 1975 saw the Vietcong rapidly expanding south. By the end of March the cities of Hue and Da Nang had both been captured, stepping-stones to Saigon itself. By April it was clear that the days of the South Vietnamese government were numbered.

A panic began within Saigon and the remaining South Vietnamese territory, as anyone who could leave the country did. Many people in South Vietnam feared that the Vietcong would deal brutally with them. The U.S. launched "Operation Frequent Wind," evacuating thousands of U.S. civilians and individuals closely associated with the South Vietnamese regime. Those who escaped to an uncertain life in the U.S. were lucky. Many tens of thousands more were unable to arrange passage out and had to await the capture of Saigon by the Communist forces.

They were right to be afraid. On April 30, 1975, the Vietcong captured Vietnam. The Vietminh began a brutal policy of "reprogramming," in which hundreds of thousands of South Vietnamese military, political, and business leaders were sent to prison camps. There they were forced to accept Communism. Conditions were often terrible, and many thousands died. Meanwhile, without the financial aid provided by the U.S., the economy of South Vietnam collapsed.

Tragically, even this period of relative peace was not to last. The violence in Vietnam had spread to neighboring Cambodia, where a Communist group called the Khmer Rouge had taken power and begun an almost unimaginable period of horror. Between 1975 and 1979 they were responsible for the deaths of nearly one fifth of the Cambodian population. In 1978, border clashes between Cambodia and Vietnam led to a war between the two countries. A Vietnamese victory put an end to the Khmer Rouge, and Vietnam would continue to occupy portions of Cambodia up until 1989.

But Vietnam's success, and their close relationship with the Soviet Union, made China nervous. Another war broke out, the Third Indochina War, in which China invaded northern Vietnam, capturing several cities. Uninterested in finding themselves bogged down in a long land war as the U.S. had done, China opted to retreat. It would, thankfully, prove the last major conflict that would be waged in Vietnam.

The fighting in Vietnam went on for so long, and took place between so many sides, it can be difficult to sort out the reasons for it. For the North Vietnamese, the war with the U.S. was only one stage in a series of conflicts that lasted throughout much of the twentieth century. They had fought the Japanese and French before the U.S. arrived. They would fight the Cambodians and Chinese afterward. For the Vietminh, the war against the U.S. was one of national liberation, to create a united Vietnam run by the Vietnamese. Of course, the hundreds of thousands of South Vietnamese who took up arms to defend their nation saw the conflict in very different terms. For them, it was a life-and-death struggle to ensure their country wasn't overtaken by Communism, and their defeat was tragic.

Today, finally, Vietnam is a country at peace. Relations between Vietnam and America are generally good. Trade and tourism between the two countries is common. That said, human rights issues remain a concern in Vietnam. The government is controlled by the Communist Party, and freedom of speech and expression are limited.

If the Vietnamese can point clearly to why the war was necessary, the same cannot be said for many in the U.S. Debate still rages over the reasons why more than fifty thousand American soldiers died in Southeast Asia. The years following the Vietnam War are stark evidence of the untruth of Kennedy's fear of the domino theory. Though Vietnam, Cambodia, and China were all technically Communist countries, this did not stop them from engaging in combat against one another. There was never any realistic possibility of a united Communist force in Southeast Asia. National interests still dominated strategic decision-making. In fact, the loss of Vietnam proved a relatively minor setback in the Cold War conflict. It did not strengthen the Soviet Union particularly, nor weaken the balance of power in Europe, or throughout the rest of the world.

All the same, the defeat of South Vietnam was difficult for the people of the United States to understand. For those who had been against the war, it demanded reconsideration of America's foreign policy and of its role in the world. For those who still believed that Vietnam had been a war worth fighting, the refusal of the American public to stand behind the military was a source of great shame. Even now, mention of the conflict brings out strong feelings for those who lived through it, a wound that has never entirely healed.

TIMELINE

- **1890:** Ho Chi Minh is born

- **1901:** Ngo Dinh Diem is born

- **1908:** Lyndon B. Johnson is born

- **1914:** William Westmoreland is born

- **1917:** John F. Kennedy is born

- **1923:** Henry Kissinger is born

- **1950:** American military advisors visit South Vietnam

- **1954:** Geneva Conference is held; Vietnam is split into South Vietnam and North Vietnam

- **1956:** General election is held to elect a leader of the state of Vietnam (North and South)

- **1960:** JFK is elected president of the United States

- **1963:** Ngo Dinh Diem is assassinated; John F. Kennedy is assassinated; Lyndon B. Johnson becomes U.S. president

- **1965:** U.S. begins an aerial bombing campaign in Vietnam; U.S. sends troops to South Vietnam

- **1968:** Tet Offensive is launched
- **1973:** Paris Peace Accords signed, ending U.S. involvement in Vietnam
- **1975:** Saigon falls and war is declared over
- **1976:** North and South Vietnam merge to form the Socialist Republic of Vietnam

GLOSSARY

Ally: a person or country that is on the same side during a war or disagreement

Buddhist: a person who believes in the teachings of Buddha

Capitalism: a way of organizing a country's economy so that most of the land, houses, factories, and other property belong to individuals and private companies rather than to the government

Catholic: a member of the Roman Catholic Church

Civil service: the branch of a government that takes care of the business of running a state but that does not include the lawmaking branch, the military, or the court system

Communism: a way of organizing the economy of a country so that all land, property, businesses, and resources belong to the government or community, and the profits are shared by all

Democratic: belonging to or connected with the Democratic Party, one of the two main political parties in the United States

Developing country: a country in which most people are poor and there is not yet much industry

Emigration: the act of leaving your home country to live in another country

Exile: a situation in which you are forbidden to live in your own country

Geopolitical: a combination of political and geographic factors relating to a state

Guerilla war: a war consisting of members of small groups of fighters or soldiers that often launch surprise attacks against an official army

Liberal: in favor of political change and reform

Nationalist: someone who is very proud of his or her country, or who wants to be independent

Nazi: a member of the political group led by Adolf Hitler that ruled Germany from 1933 to 1945

Nuclear weapon: a dangerous weapon that uses the power created by splitting atoms

Pope: the head of the Roman Catholic Church

Rural: of or having to do with the countryside, country life, or farming

Regime: a government that rules a people during a specific period of time

Republican: belonging to or connected with the Republican Party, one of the two main political parties in the United States

BIBLIOGRAPHY

BOOKS

Karnow, Stanley. *Vietnam, a History.* New York: Viking, 1983. Print.

Isaacson, Walter. *Kissinger: A Biography.* New York: Simon & Schuster, 1992. Print.

Goodwin, Doris Kearns. *Lyndon Johnson and the American Dream.* New York: Harper & Row, 1976. Print.

Reeves, Richard. *President Kennedy: Profile of Power.* New York: Simon & Schuster. 1993. Print.

"Life of John F. Kennedy." *John F. Kennedy Presidential Library & Museum.* Web. 14 Apr. 2012. http://www.jfklibrary.org/JFK/Life-of-John-F-Kennedy.aspx?p=3.

Duiker, William J. *Ho Chi Minh: A Life.* New York: Hyperion, 2000. Print.

Palling, Bruce. "General William Westmoreland." *The Guardian.* Guardian News and Media, 19 July 2005. Web. 14 Apr. 2012. http://www.guardian.co.uk/news/2005/jul/20/guardianobituaries.artsobituaries.

Whitney, Craig and Pace, Eric. "William C. Westmoreland Is Dead at 91; General Led U.S. Troops in Vietnam." *The New York Times.* 19, July 2005. Web. 14 Apr. 2012. http://www.nytimes.com/2005/07/19/international/asia/19westmoreland.html?pagewanted=all

"Ngo Dinh Diem (Vietnamese Political Leader)." *Encyclopedia Britannica Online.* Encyclopedia Britannica. Web. 14 Apr. 2012. http://www.britannica.com/EBchecked/topic/413521/Ngo-Dinh-Diem.

INDEX

ALSO AVAILABLE

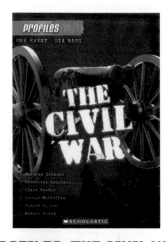

PROFILES: THE CIVIL WAR
978-0-545-23756-7

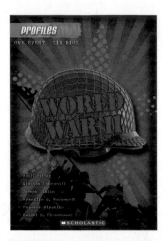

PROFILES: WORLD WAR II
978-0-545-31655-2

PROFILES: TECH TITANS
978-0-545-36577-2

PROFILES: FREEDOM HEROINES
978-0-545-42518-6